The Burden of Memories

Janet Calcaterra

Publisher's note: This book is a work of fiction. Names, characters, places and incidents are either the product of the author's imagination or are used fictitiously, and any resemblance to actual persons living or dead is entirely coincidental.

Library and Archives Canada Cataloguing in Publication

Title: The burden of memories : a novel / Janet Calcaterra.
Names: Calcaterra, Janet, author.
Identifiers: Canadiana 20210376104 | ISBN 9781988989457 (softcover)
Classification: LCC PS8605.A4543 B87 2022 | DDC C813/.6—dc23

Printed and bound in Canada on 100% recycled paper.
Cover Design: Heather Campbell
Author photo: Liz Lott

Published by:
Latitude 46 Publishing
info@latitude46publishing.com
Latitude46publishing.com

We acknowledge the support of the Ontario Arts Council, the Government of Canada and the Ontario Media Development Corporation for their generous support.

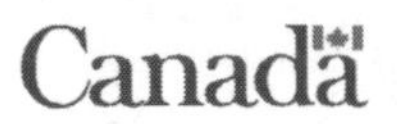

The Burden of Memories

Janet Calcaterra

With love and thanks to my family

Report from Ortona

". . . neither in this war nor the last, nor in any other, has there been anything more bitter and intense."

Matthew Halton, CBC War Correspondent

"Dwell on the beauty of life. Watch the stars, and see yourself running with them."

Marcus Aurelius

"To live is to suffer, to survive is to find some meaning in the suffering."

Friedrich Nietzsche

See Glossary of Military Abbreviations page 198

October 15, 1938

Gloria gave me this diary to help me keep track of my life when I left her and her parents in London. She wants me to write things that happen while I'm studying medicine at the University of Toronto. Writing in a diary helps her understand her feelings, and she thinks it will also help me. She promises to never ask to read what I write, and I'll do the same for her.

Living here is a big change from living at home while I took my undergrad at Western. Mother has always had hired help. When I first got to Toronto, I had off-campus room and board and watery soup every night. Some of my classmates are in the same situation, so we rented a house near campus and hired a housekeeper to clean, do the laundry, and cook. We play poker, drink, and attend class when we're not hung over. I need more money from Father, or I must quit losing at cards.

There are lots of beautiful women here, but none as lovely as Gloria.

I'm friends with Tom MacPhee, who's first in class. It's useless to study as he always beats me, but I beat him at chess.

George MacPherson invited me home to Ottawa for the weekend. He lives in a big house with maids, like home. His father works in a government ministry. George said, "I'll introduce you to everybody who's anybody." Big deal, who's anybody? George's father is important, but so's mine — even if it's only in London and he owns a hardware store.

ONE

Adrienne

Adrienne's headache pounds like the sleet on her roof. From under the covers, she hears her bedside phone ring. The sound startles her, making her head throb harder. She fumbles for the receiver and misses, knocking a lamp to the floor. Ignoring it, she burrows back under the duvet. Finally, the machine answers. Later, she opens her eyes and sees green-fluorescent digits glaring 1:00 p.m. She can almost hear the clock scold "hangover," but tries, through the pain, to retrieve the message.

"I called to ask you for lunch, but someone at your work said you'd lost your job," her mother says. "What happened, and what will you do?" As if she expects an answer, a five-year plan bordered in blue — something Adrienne could produce if she still had an assistant. "Don't do anything foolish," she adds, and the machine clicks off.

Adrienne tries to imagine what "anything foolish" means, but she's pretty sure Gloria is saying "Don't get so drunk you can't stand up and forget to set the alarm, like you did when Graham left." She waits for five minutes in case the phone rings again. When it doesn't, she struggles up and calculates a path to the bathroom.

After the Director of Human Resources escorted her out of the building with her box of belongings, Tuesday morning, she'd shut the door, taken one unopened bottle and one partial bottle of scotch and a glass from the liquor cabinet, placed them in a large cloth bag with a package of tissues, her sterling silver bookends, and her favourite fountain pen — rescued from the office — and the mail that had been building in the box by the front door. Then, she headed upstairs to her bedroom, tears already washing her cheeks. She'd managed to hold them back, while leaving work, by squeezing her eyes shut and biting, hard, inside her cheek, but once home, the water flowed onto her white silk shirt with the force of a light spring rain.

She'd sat on the side of her bed, mopped her face with the tissues, poured some scotch into the glass from the partial bottle, and started drinking. Her hope was to erase the image of her trench-coated self, carrying her worldly goods in two shopping bags while aimlessly wandering downtown streets. Between crying bouts and sips of scotch, she spent time wondering what she'd do without the job that had filled her whole life, and, indeed, what she'd done to lose it.

Although the Human Resources Director gave no explanation for her dismissal, which she thinks may be against the law, she'll decide what to do about that later. She could guess it was their disagreement about the firm's charity work, but she can't summon any energy to care about that now. The other possibility might be that she hadn't worked to build her client base, yet she can't change history. Regardless of the reasons, the loss was huge for her as everyone she could call a friend, except her fellow stargazers, worked there, and her social life revolved around them. At the end of a work day, she'd often go out for dinner with whoever was still in the office. On Friday nights, she'd go to a movie if any of those friends were up for it. And, when the firm sponsored a fundraising event, she and her colleagues would arrive together to whatever they'd arranged: a play, a musical, a ball, or maybe a trip. Buying clothes for these often-formal occasions filled her time, and wearing them made her feel beautiful.

Besides spending time at work with her colleagues, she'd always felt rewarded by helping people invest their money and watching it grow. When her father died, the insurance he left had provided essentials for his family, but many of the luxuries she'd had while growing up came from her paternal grandparents. When her mother worried about things like paying the house taxes or her daughters' university tuition, her father's family stepped in. This left her mother feeling indebted to them.

Wanting to avoid any such problems in her own life, Adrienne took finance at university, which taught her about investing for herself and others. When she fully realized, between crying spurts, what she'd lost in losing her job — her friends, her social life, and her purpose — she'd turned to the only thing she could think of for comfort. She changed into a nightgown and crawled into bed, pulling the duvet over her head. After she slept until it was dark outside the bedroom window, she sat on the bed's edge and leisurely drank, then slept again and finally watched TV, slumped against makeup-smeared pillows. She woke to a grumbling stomach, reminding her she hadn't eaten for days, and the only place she'd gone was from her bed to the bathroom.

Now, she steps gingerly around the mess on her bedroom floor, including dropped clothes and shoes, her open briefcase with its papers strewn over the carpet, the empty bottles of scotch, and heads toward the bathroom again. Weak from hunger, her knees wobble as she walks. She notices, with her foot poised above her cast-off suit, Tuesday's mail under the red-wool fabric. Before she can stop herself, she steps down on an overstuffed XPRESSPOST package and hears cardboard crunch. She clears a path for her return trip by kicking the obstacles aside and looks forward to the oblivion of bed and more sleep.

Taking a bottle of aspirin and some milk-of-magnesia from the cabinet above the sink, she lifts her head to swallow the pills and the mirror looks back. What she sees is not a forty-six-year-old woman who looks more like thirty-six, not the highest paid, most fashionably dressed financial planner at the firm where she'd worked for over twenty years, and definitely not someone who'd dreamed of having an extraordinary life. Rather, there's a rumpled female in an unwashed nightgown, with bloodshot eyes set above dark bags of skin, peering through chin-length strands of greasy brown hair. She pushes it behind her ears and knows she needs a tint and trim. Finding time won't be hard as Jessica, her former assistant, will have cancelled all her meetings. Tears form again as she thinks of missing enjoyable, news-filled encounters with familiar clients.

On her way back to bed, she stares out the window at her Toronto neighbourhood. Two-and-a-half storey Edwardian-style homes of somber grey brick line either side of the road. Sleet slices the sky and freezes on the ground. A mother, who's slipping with each step, drags two children in a sleigh, grocery bags tucked around them. Their fuchsia snowsuits are the one bright spot in this streetscape. She draws a corduroy throw cushion to her chest, gets into her king-sized bed, and pulls the covers back over her head. There in the dark, she's reminded by the woman and children, yet again, of the life she's always wanted but never had.

Muffled banging disturbs her dreams. The doorbell rings, then rings again.

From her upstairs bedroom, she hears, "Adrienne Adams, let me in!"

Her mother is pounding on the door and shouting her name. Anyone in the street can hear this display. She covers her head with her pillow and hopes none of her neighbours are out in the freezing rain. Her bed is safe and warm. She drifts in and out of sleep. The banging stops, but soon it starts again.

Footsteps sound on the stairs, and a man's voice shouts, "Adrienne, Adrienne."

The security alarm startles her, and she's stunned by the overhead light. She sits up quickly then feels dizzy. Her mother stands next to the bed, icy water dripping from her hat. Adrienne doesn't remember her ever looking this frightened.

A man in a track suit hovers behind her.

He glances at the empty bottles and shouts over the alarm, "What else did you take?"

"What's wrong mother?" Adrienne mouths, then taps Gloria's arm to get her attention. "Who *is* this man?"

"Speak louder," her mother says.

The man approaches Adrienne and asks, "Who does your system?"

"SecurAll," she says then points to the phone. "The number's there."

He plugs his left ear to hear with his right, and she hopes he can stop the police. When the wailing finally finishes, she knows her security people have believed him

"Thank God you're okay," Gloria yells over the now-silent alarm.

"Did you think losing my job would kill me?"

"You had lots to drink."

Gloria's voice is still high-pitched as she nods at the empty bottles on the rug. Then she lays her coat on the bed.

"Only one and a half bottles after I lost my job. What did you think?"

"Get up. Eat. And stop drinking," says the man. "That way I won't have to come back."

She staggers out of bed and feels her mother staring at her diaphanous nightgown.

Gloria hands her a robe and says, "Cover up."

"Who is this guy?"

"Anthony Nardi, the retired policeman John hired to help me."

"Please, call me Tony," he says to Adrienne.

As his salt-and-pepper-coloured hair is the only sign of age on this man, she thinks he looks too young to be retired.

"Why did you break in?" Adrienne asks her mother, noting her anxious look.

"I phoned, and you didn't answer. I rang your bell, and you didn't answer. When Tony rang it and you didn't answer, he broke in. I was worried about you, your job. Your father . . . disappointments always affected him badly."

Her mother never speaks of her father, who died when she was twelve, and she's never seen her stepfather react badly to disappointment, so Adrienne is puzzled by this.

Before she can ask what her mother means, Gloria says, "Oh, I meant your stepfather. You know men. John hates to lose. He gets so upset." None of this makes any sense to Adrienne, but she feels too hungover to ask for clarification.

"I'm finished," Tony says. Adrienne hears the door close and knows he's gone.

"Don't embarrass me like that again," Gloria says, wagging her index figure.

"Me embarrass you? You broke into my house!"

"I was afraid." Gloria's face still looks frightened. "When does your housekeeper come?"

"You mean Clara? Monday."

"Could she come tomorrow?"

"No, Mother. I don't know how to be polite about this, so butt out!"

Gloria grimaces but says nothing and reaches for the XPRESSPOST envelope on the floor.

"Leave that for Clara."

"The return address says your Aunt Margaret. But she doesn't live in London."

"She moved back from Calgary before Christmas. That's her new address. We keep in touch."

"You could have told me. Just because she and I don't write doesn't mean I'm not interested in hearing how she is. And don't think telling me you're in touch with Margaret will hurt my feelings," Gloria says, her mouth tight.

"Oh Mother," Adrienne sighs in frustration.

Gloria places the envelope and the other mail on the desk then turns to feel her daughter's forehead.

"Where are you going all dressed up?" Adrienne asks.

"A play at the Tarragon. You know, that little theatre. John's picking me up here. We're meeting Lucie and Arthur. How long since you've eaten?"

"Breakfast on my last day of work."

"A few days ago? No wonder you can't get up. You're weak from hunger. I'll make you something," and she gathers the bottles from the floor and strides off.

Soon Adrienne stares at a bowl of split-pea soup. Its salty smell makes her want to bolt for the bathroom, but instead, she counts to ten then starts eating. Gloria watches from the armchair, reminding Adrienne of the winter when she was sixteen and had mononucleosis. Her mother read Frances Parkinson Keyes's novels aloud to her, day after day, as if the tales of far-off France would transport her daughter to health. When she's finished eating, her head feels clearer.

Gloria takes the tray, saying, "You need groceries. Your cupboards are bare."

"I don't. Because I eat in restaurants."

"I know you've got savings. You could probably retire, but in case you don't get a job right away, maybe you shouldn't blow money on eating out."

"We'll see. Now call John or you'll miss the play."

She turns on the porch light and watches her mother manoeuvre her way down the icy steps while John shuffles up the walk, calling, "Wait. I'll help." When he reaches Gloria, he takes her purse, and they link arms.

"*Merda*," he scolds. "It's really icy here," and they totter down the walk together.

Adrienne closes the door and smiles at John's favourite Italian invective. Now that she's eaten, she thinks she should have a digestive, like a little sherry or a liqueur — her usual habit and the proper end to a meal. After all, she did just lose her job. She switches on the chandelier and looks in the dining room's liquor cabinet. She knows she's drunk most of the scotch, but all she can see is bar paraphernalia in the cabinet. Two shot glasses, a corkscrew, a bottle opener, and a variety of glassware grace the back of the cupboard. To the left is an untouched bottle of cola. To the right is an ice bucket. All alcohol has disappeared.

Her mother had picked up both scotch bottles as she left the bedroom, one with a swig still left in it. It had taken her the day she was fired, then a night of slow drinking, and then another day to finish them, which not only gave her a hangover but also made her vomit. Now, with nothing else to do, she's ready for another drink, but all of the bottles she and Graham had accumulated for entertaining are gone. Her first thought is that they were in her mother's purse, but wouldn't she have heard the bottles clinking as she walked?

She checks the garbage in the kitchen. It's topped with empty bottles and the sink smells like a brewery. Her mother must have poured the last swig of scotch down the drain while she heated the soup. The idea that Gloria disposed of all her booze hits Adrienne, making her angry. Will her mother ever stop interfering?

Although she'd prefer sherry or a liqueur, if any of the bottles of alcohol were there, she'd drink one of them in a pinch. She holds the wall and slides to the floor, sitting cross-legged as her bare feet grow cold. A drink would lift her spirits, but there's nothing to pour, so she starts making coffee in the kitchen. As it drips, she goes upstairs and finds the birthday slippers her sister, Cass, sent last year. Usually, she wears nylons in the house, not bothering to change after work, but these moccasins will warm her feet and remind her of Cass's caring nature, which is something Adrienne could use in abundance right now.

Back in the kitchen with her daybook, she marvels how it's already January 1995. The older she gets the faster time passes. She sits down with a coffee and the cordless phone. If her mother's play was over, Adrienne would call Gloria and John and scold them for stealing her booze, but because their phone doesn't take messages, she can't record a rebuke. She looks in her daybook for where she's jotted her colleagues' numbers. Although she doesn't really need the money, maybe one of them will know of a job she could get. Working would keep her busy and useful.

A voice mail greets her each time she dials. They're probably out together for the evening.

One message, "Sorry, I can't come to the phone right now. I'm out doing business," makes her laugh out loud. She decides, after what feels like a communal brush off from her co-workers, not to call anyone until she can say she has a job. She could look for a liquor store that's open Friday nights or go to a tavern and get tanked, but the only Toronto bar she's gone to in years is the one where she used to have a drink with colleagues after work and where her firm had its Christmas party. She decides it's probably too upscale for getting drunk, so she flicks on the kitchen TV and searches for the Dial-a-Bottle ad. Delivery is the answer. She's about to phone and order her brand of scotch to be delivered when, next to the ad, her horoscope flashes on the screen.

About Capricorn, the writing says, "You'll be in fine form this week. The future beckons."

Fine form? After non-stop, day-and-night drinking, her skull, teeth, arms, and even fingernails ache. Still, getting buzzed would soothe her shame at being fired. She calls in an order to the taxi company for a large bottle of scotch. That way, there'll be no reason to go out in the morning.

She wakes with her head on the kitchen table when she hears banging on the door. It's the cab driver with her bottle. She could take a drink up to her third-floor observatory and look at the stars, but freezing rain still ravages the roof. Even if she could see the planets through the storm, she wouldn't find her constellation in this January sky. More than anything, what she really needs is sleep.

On her way to bed, she sees Aunt Margaret's XPRESSPOST envelope on the bedroom desk. She crosses the room and breaks the seal with a letter opener. The contents spill out, and two items fall to the floor. One is a translucent-blue aerogram. The other is a note scribbled in pencil on a scrap of cheap lined paper. The aerogram has a post-it note stuck to it from Aunt Margaret saying, "You may want to read these old letters your father sent from the war." Although she worries that reading them might bring back the sadness she'd felt for so long after his death, she pulls the note away and sees a code-like return address on the aerogram. The back says, "PASSED BY CENSOR No. 1187." She begins to read.

ROCCA SAN GIOVANNI 09-12-43
5th Field Ambulance
1st Can. Div.
R.C.A.M.C.

Dear Mother and Father,
Your letter, which came yesterday, was the quickest I've received at the front. More than nine months have passed, but your cable about Gloria's stillbirth has never come. She looked so forward to the baby, but now she's alone, and I'm still trying to deal with my sadness. I wonder what else I've missed.
Love, Alex

While she knew her mother was so secretive about her own life that she sometimes seemed cold and unfeeling, reading that she'd had a stillborn baby evoked compassion for her. It must have been almost unbearable, while her husband was at war so early in their marriage, to lose a child whose arrival she'd longed for. Considering this saddened Adrienne and made her admit that when she was trying to get pregnant, Gloria was able to put aside painful memories and encourage her daughter to "keep trying" because she, herself, had had two successful pregnancies after that stillbirth.

Adrienne pushes away the pain of recalling how she was unable to conceive with Graham and retrieves the other note from the floor. Although it was written by her father while at war, she doesn't expect, as she reads, for anything written in pencil on cheap, lined paper, torn from a school scribbler, to be very consequential.

1959

Mother,
You've always understood me. The girls are doing well. Today, I lost my battle-fatigue patients at the hospital, and we could use this money. It would help if Gloria could teach, but she can't. Married women aren't allowed in the classroom, as if their carnal knowledge

might rub off on the children. Besides, if she could return to teaching, people would think I couldn't provide for my family. In order to do that now, I'll have to look for more patients in need of psychiatry.

When I'm alone in the den, I can't stop thinking about the dead. It's as if they're calling me to join them.
Alex

On reading this, Adrienne is stunned at how she'd presumed, so flippantly, that anything her father might have written, even thirty-six years ago, would be inconsequential. After all, he was a medical doctor who'd studied to become a psychiatrist after the war, so he must have been intelligent, if not insightful. She wishes she also had that gift of insight regarding this letter. It puzzles her enough that she's curious about what he meant by the dead. Maybe it has something to do with the war.

Finally, after much reflection, she returns to the letters, hoping as she reads them, they'll tell her more about what he was both feeling and thinking when he wrote those puzzling lines. She's always known he studied psychiatry at the University of Toronto and then practiced it. Her memory says he wore a navy, double-breasted wool suit with a pipe in his pocket when he went to the hospital to advise patients. That's not how she sees him as an army doctor. She knows that in the midst of bombs falling, while practicing medicine in combat zones, he'd have worn an army uniform, probably with a white gown covering it. She also doubts Cass knows their mother had another child, born dead, and considering Gloria's tight lips, she bets John doesn't know either. Not that it matters whether she told him about something that happened years ago.

While staring at the pile of old letters, Adrienne thinks she can smell stale tobacco. Maybe he smoked as he wrote these. When she remembers him, it's with a pipe between his teeth and a drink next to him. He would read the newspaper in the living room. Behind him, a streetlamp would shine through a crack in the cabbage-rose drapes. He'd fall asleep with his chin on his chest, snoring, his pipe no longer lit. Hardly a man with a tortured soul.

Among the letters, she recognizes one on Aunt Margaret's stationary and pulls it out.

Suite 115, Leisuretyme
London, Ont.
December 24, 1994

Dear Adrienne,

A brief note to tell you I'm safely moved. While packing, I found these letters and war memorabilia your grandmother saved from your father's life, and I thought you should have them. The only time I heard him talk about the war was one night, after he returned, when we had dinner at our parents' house. From a map of Italy, he showed our mother where they were written. She printed the towns in capital letters next to the return addresses. After dessert, he and mother reread them, and he cried. The letters are informative, and I hope you'll find them interesting. I know I saved a diary, somewhere, that he wrote while he was at war. I think he sent it to me so Gloria wouldn't read it. When I unpack it, I'll send that, too. Write soon.
Love,
Aunt Margaret

She places the papers in an empty chocolate box she finds in her closet and sets it on her desk to look at later. Feeling grubby from three days without washing, she goes to the bathroom and sits on the bathtub's edge. Her legs feel like folded paper, and she doesn't have the energy to turn on the tap. Rain pelts the window. Her room is so dark that clouds must be covering the moon. The stars don't offer any navigational tools tonight.

April 12, 1942

This is only the second time I've written in this journal. I've been too busy with med school assignments and the odd letter.

I've almost finished interning, which was shortened so doctors could go overseas. Gloria and I are getting married at the farm on Dominion Day with a picnic supper. I love her laugh, and Margaret thinks we should marry. I hope Gloria doesn't get as obsessed with our social status as mother is.

Med school is rewarding. I wanted to farm, but Father said I was too smart to grow tobacco. I love the outdoors but think medicine will keep my mind occupied. Mother said, "Your friends will be impressed about your being a doctor." The other students, like Tom MacPhee, are so smart about medicine — anatomy, circulation, physiology — I'm afraid they'll get ahead, so I study harder.

I've learned how to play chess, become a better golfer, and practiced piano on the upright in this old house. I've also sung in U. of T's. Men's Chorus, but playing piano is more fun than singing, probably because once I've heard a tune, I can pick it up on the piano immediately.

TWO

Gloria

John leans on the doorframe between the kitchen and dining room and asks, "Why do we need to get Adrienne's groceries?"

"She doesn't have any food in the house, and I'm afraid if she goes out, she'll visit the liquor store. Remember how she drank after Graham left?"

"She's forty-six," he says and turns to pick up cups from the dining room table. "And I don't think losing a job is the same as losing a husband, even if he couldn't accept that she was better at sales. Her heart was broken when he left. Besides, we can't control her."

"Forty-seven on Monday. We should celebrate her birthday," Gloria says. "It might lift her spirits." She returns to the dining room and carries a bowl of stewed prunes to the refrigerator in the kitchen. "And I want to get her eating."

Although she wishes John would change into something more fashionable, Gloria knows his worn dress pants and multi-coloured pullover from another era are his excuse for comfort. She could suggest he change, but, not wanting to offend him, she keeps her thoughts to herself.

"Did you think throwing out the bottles after pouring what was left in them down the sink would get her eating?"

"You should've seen how much she drank."

She hands him a tray for the remaining dishes, which he'd carried to the kitchen every day throughout their twenty-five years of marriage. It was simpler to clear the table from the breakfast nook of the Rosedale home where she'd lived with Alex, but John wouldn't move from Woodbridge to that "uptight" neighbourhood, and she wouldn't leave her beloved Toronto, so they sold both properties and bought this condo near the theatre district.

John covers the counter with dishes then retreats to the dining room, where he eases into a chair, wincing from the arthritis pain in his knee.

"I guess this bad news has caused Adrienne to drink like she did when Graham left," he says.

She waits a minute then says, "Maybe, but even after he left, she always had work. She couldn't drink heavily and still be the top salesperson in her office."

"Don't worry. She'll get another job."

Gloria is so tired she can hardly keep her thoughts straight, let alone consider her daughter's job prospects. She takes a deep breath and continues with, "I'm afraid Adrienne will do something drastic."

"You mean like retire?"

"She could probably afford to retire, but she's young, and I think she'd be bored. Besides, women live much longer now. She might need the money later. Now, let's go."

He pushes in his chair, and she hears the hall closet slide open. When the phone rings, she knows it's her daughter, Cassandra, calling from North Bay. She calls every Saturday just as they're leaving for the market. Straining to listen, Gloria hears John whisper to Cass about Adrienne's job. Then he passes her the receiver while his hand still covers it.

"Get your coat," she whispers, knowing that if she doesn't talk now, Cass will call Adrienne and say she's sick. "I'll be finished in a second," she says and takes the phone. Without stopping to greet Cass, she scolds, "I've told you. On Saturday mornings we go shopping."

As if ignoring her mother, Cass asks, "How's Adrienne?"

"She's lost her job, so she's been in bed for days."

Gloria remembers how Adrienne, hung over, missed several days' work when Graham left. Finally, her love for her job took over and she went back, more ambitious than ever. But she can't do that now. She doesn't have a job to return to.

"Sounds bad. Send her here for Reading Week. We'll go shopping in Sudbury. Eaton's has good underwear, which I need, and there isn't one in North Bay."

"Why don't you both come to Florida?"

"Sam's got school in February."

"What about March break? Samantha could come then," Gloria says, although she doubts she has the energy for a week with a teenager, even if Sam *is* her granddaughter.

"That's *not* going to happen," Cass says. "Sam has a break, but the university doesn't. I have to teach. Now go to the market."

Gloria hangs up, feeling frustrated that Cass and Sam can't just visit her from where Cass used to live in Toronto rather than having to fly or drive for four hours. She's never really forgiven Cass for moving to northern Ontario, pregnant and without her husband, Eric. And all to be a professor. She pats her silver curls in the mirror and tries to cheer herself with a smile, tight though it is.

John opens the door and steps into the hall, saying, "I'll bring the car around."

She applies blush and lipstick and tones them with a tissue. As she pulls on her coat, she checks the mirror again and reassures herself that, at seventy-one, she still looks attractive. Downstairs through the lobby window, Gloria sees Thomas, the doorman, spreading salt on the walk. John steers the Volvo around the driveway from the parking garage. She watches him stop near the building's door and shuffle toward Thomas, then grab his arm. They hit rock-salted ice, teeter forward and stand upright. John opens the lobby door and Thomas is right behind him.

"I'll have the groceries delivered so we don't have to go out," she says.

"What about Adrienne?" Beneath his corduroy cap, she sees his face, strained with concern.

"You're right," she says and asks Thomas to call a cab while John puts the car back in the garage.

From the taxi, Gloria watches a woman in a yellow raincoat slip on the sidewalk, coated with freezing rain.

"*Merda*," John says. "What awful weather. We should have stayed home. But taking Adrienne groceries will give us a chance to see how she is."

Gloria recognizes John's imperative lawyer's voice. While his favourite swear word is not as vulgar as some others, she dislikes this colourful language as much as his outdated clothes. He probably got into the habit of speaking crudely during World War II, as Alex had, although neither talked much about the war.

Over the years, she's tried not to mention her first husband, not wanting John to feel threatened by thinking that Alex had been more suitable than he. Only recently, he'd told Gloria how, because of his Italian parents, he'd been interned at the beginning of WWII near Pembroke, Ontario as a fascist sympathizer. Then he was conscripted. This information shocked her, but today she's so tired her mind is shifting rapidly from one thought to another. Soon, John's last name, Renzetti, bubbles up. She recalls how it caused talk among her WASP friends when she married him. If they ever hear of how he was detained, their dinner party invitations might cease. When she thinks about that part of his life, she doesn't have to remember Alex's faults to feel awkward about both of her husbands.

Familiar aromas of smoked meat, seafood, and cheese fill the market building; Gloria hears vendors' voices, like circus barkers, drift out of shop stalls, enticing passersby with their wares. She takes mesh bags from her purse and hands some to John.

"Get Adrienne some old cheddar and —"

"Okay," he says. "But no meat or chicken, and she'll eat eggs and fish."

"Yes. So we should take some of everything she likes," Gloria says. "We need to get her eating."

"We'll do that," says John, and he squeezes her elbow affectionately. "I think she says she's vegetarian, and might not eat meat just to irk you, but you can't make her eat what she doesn't want."

"Then we need to get her some prepared food."

"Let's get bread, vegetables, fruit, a deli dish or two. Then I have to check on the soup kitchen delivery."

Gloria is proud that John has a generous heart and used his resources to start this charity to feed the hungry.

"You go that way." She points right. "Meet you at noon."

Turning left, she examines bins of dried beans, grains, and pasta, but she's distracted, thinking about yesterday. She'd almost told Adrienne how much Alex was drinking before he died. To herself, she calls him an alcoholic, but she'd never used that word about the girls' father with anyone else. She'd intended to tell her daughters, when they were old enough, how their father drank too much, but the right time never came. To think of it, that information might explain Adrienne's habit now.

After she remarried, Gloria was afraid that if the girls knew about their father's addiction, they'd tell John. She didn't want John to know how Alex turned to alcohol after the war, when life wasn't what he expected. And, as his wife, there was nothing she could do to cure his illness. John had once told her he thought people who used alcohol to dull their feelings were weak. This was probably an explanation for his own heavy drinking after his return from the war before he kicked the habit.

Abruptly, she realizes if she doesn't hurry and finish her shopping, John will ask what's bothering her again. She moves on, tasting the odd cold cut or pickle as she buys groceries. Then, wanting to forget yesterday at Adrienne's, she thinks about John's open-hearted acceptance of her children. When Cass took a job at the relatively unknown Nipissing University, he told Gloria he thought the position wasn't prestigious enough, but he didn't say so to Cass. After Adrienne and Graham divorced, because Gloria had mixed feelings about their split, John kept quiet again. She believes this hands-off approach helped her daughters feel close to him. Something Gloria had wanted when they married.

When they have bought all they need at the big market building, they cross the road to a smaller structure in search of flowers for Adrienne. Its outside wall is painted with pictures of tomatoes and squash. Once inside, they squeeze their bags between chairs occupied by people and pass a table with four women in running suits and money belts covering their middle-aged spreads.

A pony-tailed woman reaches out and, touching John's arm, asks, "How's Adrienne?"

He stops and gestures toward the woman, saying, "Gloria, do you remember Lucille Douglas? She works in the financial sector — like Adrienne."

Gloria nods and says, "Nice to see you again."

"Adrienne's okay, considering the shock," John says.

"Did you work with her?" Gloria asks.

"We weren't with the same firm," Lucille says. "We networked. As long as we weren't competing for a sale, she gave me good tips." Lucille looks like she'll introduce the whole table, so Gloria starts moving toward the egg stall.

"Nice talking to you," John says and follows Gloria.

Near the florist's booth, she asks, "Do you think, at the end, Adrienne was drinking on the job?"

"Doubtful. You said it yourself. She had to keep her head, but she didn't like selling anything the company made more from than she did. She needs her own firm. Now, what should we buy?"

"Something that says spring is coming."

Eventually, they pick daffodils, daisies, and white carnations.

John carries Adrienne's groceries up to her house while Gloria holds the flowers and backs out of the cab. Her heel catches the curb, and she stumbles, dropping the bouquet. A man jogs past on the sidewalk. Three strides beyond her he stops, turns, and picks up the flowers.

"Hello, Gloria," he says, steadying her with his hand.

She regains her balance and takes the bouquet. While cradling it in her arm, she recognizes him as Tony, the man who helped her break into Adrienne's last night.

"How is she?" he asks and nods toward the door.

"We haven't seen her yet."

He wears a frayed toque, hiding all but the bottom of his greying curls. He's over six feet, yet, despite her five-foot-two stature, Gloria doesn't feel overpowered by his height. Although she's not very good at guessing a person's age, she thinks he's about forty-five. His dark-brown eyes and square jawline make him handsome in a classic way.

"I live near here, so when John asked me to check on her, it wasn't a problem. If he needs me to, I can jog by every day and say hello."

"Maybe," Gloria says. "If he wants that, John will call you." And Tony lopes off down the street. She joins her husband on the porch where he's leaning on the railing.

"Do you want to retain Tony to watch out for Adrienne?"

"She'll pull herself together," he says, shaking his head. "Remember how long it took her to get over Graham? Still, she did eventually." The front door opens, and seeing his stepdaughter in street clothes, he looks at Gloria and bobs his head once.

"Why are you here?" Adrienne asks, blocking the doorway.

"We brought you some food."

"What about the bottles you took?"

"When you get over losing your job, I'll bring you some new ones," Gloria says. She sees up close that Adrienne's eyes are puffy, despite her makeup.

"I'll get my own, thanks. I just hate that you try to control me."

John approaches the door, and Adrienne backs up far enough to let him past. He puts her groceries in the front hall, then steps back outside.

"Lunch date?" Gloria asks.

"No, Mother."

"Enough," John says as he slices his neck with a cutting motion. "She's probably got more to do now than she had before."

I hope so, Gloria thinks and presents the bouquet, saying, "The flowers were irresistible."

"Thank you. And for the food." Adrienne moves back from the doorway, as if to invite them in. "I'll unload the groceries —

then call you a cab."

John steps into the hall again, smiling. Gloria follows him and turns to close the door when she sees Tony, looking back at them from the end of the block.

When Gloria opens the fridge to unload the food they've brought, the smell of broccoli rotting in the crisper is so strong that John exits the kitchen. Adrienne shoves the flowers into an old mayonnaise jar half filled with water and puts it on the table. Gloria, who knows her daughter received crystal vases as wedding gifts, wants to ask, "Why is your house so beautiful, but you live like a slob?" Instead, she says, "Could you make some espresso while I wipe out the crisper?"

Silently, Adrienne starts the coffee machine. She leans around the living room door and asks John, "Do you want your coffee in there or here?"

"Has your mother cleaned that smelly fridge?"

Without waiting for an answer, he starts into the kitchen. Gloria is tying the floppy brown broccoli into a plastic bag. Then she puts the crisper into a sink of soapy water.

"You're a sissy," she says to John and sits beside him.

Adrienne places demitasses of coffee on the table.

"We're concerned," he says. "We know you liked your job, but you'll find another. You're good at what you do."

Gloria gets up, hoping her silence will encourage them to talk. She dries the crisper then begins washing romaine.

"When I was sent home, it was humiliating," Adrienne says. "At least I got told in my office so no one heard. But my coworkers saw me take boxes and leave. I know they'll tell stories about how I stole clients or records. All lies. But that won't help me get another job."

"That will stop when they hear the next juicy thing. And if it doesn't, I know a few good libel lawyers who owe me favours."

His lawyer voice sounds threatening, but Gloria smiles inwardly at his helpful nature. It's one of the things she truly loves about him.

"The meeting replays in my head like a stuck record," Adrienne says. "And, to top it off, I have to figure out what to do next."

He nods once, characteristically, in agreement. "I've been there. Like when I was demobbed from the Navy after the war."

"I know you don't like to talk about it, but where were you stationed again?"

"On a minesweeper. We cleared the beach at Normandy before our troops landed."

Gloria stops dunking lettuce. The last time something came on TV about the war, they were watching together in bed, and John immediately found a Fred Astaire movie. Now, his openness makes her uneasy that he'll cry, something he once did when talking about the war. The tears seemed natural to her then, but she doesn't want any probing questions from Adrienne now in case she cries herself. She doesn't need Adrienne asking her what about the war makes her sad. To answer, she'd have to talk about Alex, and she certainly doesn't want to do that.

"Life was different when I got back to Canada," he says. "I didn't know what to do with my time, so I rented a room and took to drinking. That didn't get me anywhere. Drinking won't help you either, Adrienne."

Finally, thinks Gloria, he's come to the point: Adrienne doesn't know what to do.

"Have some more salad," she says to Adrienne, but John keeps talking.

"The day my landlady had the police break in to get her rent, I got a job in a bar. Then, with veterans' free tuition, I got my bachelor's. After that, I went into law."

"But now you're a businessman," Adrienne says and hands her empty bowl to Gloria to fill.

"Business interested me more than law, but I didn't know that until I studied it. By the time I graduated, my father had died, so I worked in my parents' construction business."

Gloria is relieved when John stops talking, so she can add, "You need to get on with your life, Adrienne."

"I was trying to do that when you turned up at my door."

"Maybe you need time to think about what you'll do next," he says.

"First I need to get the 'firing' conversation out of my head," says Adrienne, putting the second bowl of salad, untouched, on the counter. Then, she turns to Gloria and says, "Speaking of the war . . . that package from Aunt Margaret had letters Daddy wrote home from Italy."

Gloria feels her shoulders tense. Fear fills her chest as she leans against the counter. She wonders why Margaret sent those letters and what they say, then remembers the bassinette in the apartment she'd had while Alex was at war and how it remained empty, its skirt dressed with pink-and-blue cross-stitched fabric. Her throat muscles tighten.

"The one I've read mentions that stillborn baby you had while Daddy was at war. It must have been awful to go through that without him. I remember how, despite you having to relive that loss, you encouraged me to keep trying to get pregnant. But of course, by then it didn't matter anyway."

Gloria wants to say, "Graham was there to support you," but she doesn't want to remind Adrienne that she's never had children. That would be too cruel. She knows she can't allow this conversation to go on any longer, for all of their sakes, in case Alex comes up, so she puts the lettuce into a plastic bag then asks John to call a cab.

July 10, 1943

Today, my unit landed in Pachino in the south-west corner of Sicily. Landing was difficult. The landscape isn't lush like I imagined — too dry for palm trees and bougainvillea — instead, there are olive trees and barking dogs. Dust covers everything.

Got seasick in the boat from ship-to-shore, but couldn't stand up to heave over the side in case of snipers, so I vomited on the floor. Soon the stinking amphibious craft was slippery with puke. Operating on humans has never made me as nauseated as that smell . . .

Tom MacPhee, friend from U. of T., stepped from our boat onto land. His genius didn't protect him from catching a mine. He lost toes. Grant Chapman and I pulled him to safety. There was equipment in the boat, so I made a tourniquet with Grant's mother's linen handkerchief and stemmed the bleeding.

When we set out for land, Grant said water frightened him more than bullets — I stayed with him until after Tom was sent to a hospital ship offshore — by then landing easy to Grant — he is tall, muscled like I wish I were — has blonde hair — played varsity football wide receiver for Alberta — nurses swoon over him. I'd be jealous if he didn't make me laugh so goddam hard.

Right now, Sicily is like League of Nations — Italians live here — Germans occupy it — both British and American troops took beaches today — all landings met with little Sicilian resistance — as far as I know, the Jerries have fled.

THREE

Cass

Cass downshifts into third gear, urging her Miata to climb Airport Hill. All day, snow-swollen clouds from the northwest have threatened and are now letting loose large flakes that blanket the dirty snowbanks lining the road. Such flurries are a welcome break from two weeks of deepfreeze. During today's final class before Reading Week, she'd wished a blizzard would ground Adrienne's flight and her arrival would be postponed for several days. The week would pass, and Cass could return to school without Adrienne coming to North Bay.

When her sister called a month ago to say she'd bought a ticket, Cass — who'd always envied Adrienne's large Toronto home because she, herself, lived in an apartment — went into overdrive. She washed walls, ironed curtains, and waxed floors. Then she bought new furniture and rugs for her living room, as the old ones looked shabby. This spending spree, her usual way of coping with anxiety, always improved her mood until the credit card bills came, when depression enveloped her. By yesterday, she was so tired from cleaning that she felt neither physically nor emotionally prepared for Adrienne's visit, and she certainly didn't have the energy to shop for food.

As she turns into the airport, her tires slide on slush, and she reminds herself to slow down. She joins a crowd of people on the first floor opposite the runway and sees, through the glass doors, snowflakes tumble under floodlights. Soon, Adrienne stands in front of her. Cass squeals and leans forward for a hug. Her sister wears a pea jacket and denim skirt. Her normally dark brown, stylishly cut hair is scruffy and light with gray. Puffy pockets swell beneath her eyes. Adrienne's disheveled look seems to say she's depressed, and her appearance makes Cass feel overdressed in her full-length, black coat.

"Is that carry-on your only bag?" Cass asks, pointing to the small piece of luggage Adrienne's carrying.

"Yes. I thought, for an outing, we could go shopping in Sudbury."

"The only worthwhile store there is Eaton's. They have good bras and socks, and I need both."

"All I need is jeans, but we could drink scotch and watch soaps instead."

That's not going to happen, thinks Cass as she holds open the door. Until her sister was fired, Cass remembers how, years ago, Adrienne talked about being up before dawn, calling clients before coffee, eating lunch at her desk, and, without exception, dressing in business suits and tailored blouses. In short: an over-achiever. Seeing Adrienne's ragged hair confirms why their mother is worried.

"We could," Cass says, putting Adrienne's bag into her trunk. "Or we could decide later."

Snow makes the road down Airport Hill slippery. Below, Lake Nipissing is dotted with fishing huts, today's holes already frozen.

At Algonquin, Cass turns left and asks, "Was there food on the plane?"

"Peanuts and a drink. I didn't have breakfast, so I'm a bit hungry."

Great, thinks Cass. A guest with an empty stomach and a kitchen that's bare except for dried beans, brown rice, and a frozen lasagna, which all take time to cook. She wishes she'd found the energy for grocery shopping.

"I just want a drink with my feet up."

"Let's get you settled at home. Then we'll eat out and stop at the liquor store."

Cass opens her apartment's door, and her daughter Samantha

squeals, "Hello Aunt Adrienne," stretching out her arms for a hug.

"You look more like your aunt than you do me, your own mother."

"I've heard that before," Sam says. Her hair is pulled back into a ponytail, accentuating her heart-shaped face.

"I wish," Adrienne says. "Oh for that unwrinkled skin."

"We were going to eat out, but you've already eaten," Cass says and points to the half-finished bowl of cereal on the table.

"Just a snack. I'll go brush my teeth."

"While you're at it, could you show your aunt her room?"

As Sam and Adrienne disappear down the hall, Cass wipes the table, loads the dishwasher, and cleans off the counter. She wonders how things get so messy with only two people living there, but she doesn't want Adrienne to think she's a slob. After all, it *is* her first visit to North Bay.

When Cass moved north from Toronto, Adrienne would never use her precious vacation days to visit what she thought was wilderness. Because of this, they rarely saw each other, which made them feel like strangers. Although her mother came up for Sam's birth, she never forgave Cass for choosing work in North Bay over marriage and living in Toronto. Because Gloria finally insisted, Cass brought four-year-old Sam to Toronto for Christmas. Since then, they've continued to visit Gloria and John in Toronto, gone to Florida the odd time at her mother's expense, and were planning to visit John's cottage in Muskoka this summer. Adrienne has often joined them for these family times.

As she finishes tidying the kitchen, Adrienne joins her and asks, "Do you mind if I look around?"

Because of the time and money she'd spent preparing for this visit, Cass proudly says, "Go ahead," and Adrienne wanders into the living room.

"I bet you sewed these Roman blinds yourself," she says. "If you bought a house, you could decorate everything."

"I'd love a house," Cass says and joins Adrienne in the dining room alcove. "But first I need a down payment, and after that, a mortgage is long-term commitment."

She knows these reasons for her not buying a house are only partly true. In his emails, the communication he prefers, Sam's father says he dreams of them settling on Vancouver Island. Despite Adrienne often calling her negative, Cass can't imagine Eric giving up his International Red Cross life. Yet, as she sits on the couch and motions for Adrienne to use the chair, she secretly hopes he'll return to Canada, for Sam's sake.

"Even if you don't live in North Bay forever, a house is a good investment."

"It'd be good for Sam, too."

From the hall Sam asks, "Are you talking about me again?"

"We just can't stop. Could you please keep your aunt company while I change? Then we'll go and eat."

In her bedroom, Cass changes, then checks her email, hoping Eric has sent a message. Thankfully, Nipissing's IT department set it up in both her office and home. That way, she can work from her apartment when she doesn't have classes or office hours. She and Eric, as Ph.D students, had married for more student aid. After graduation, they'd looked for a country where he could work and she could teach. When that didn't happen, he took a job with the Red Cross and, without realizing she was pregnant, she started teaching at Nipissing. With Sam now fourteen, Cass wonders whether she and Eric would still be together if she'd followed him. As neither wanted a divorce when they parted, Cass decided to never give up on Eric, if not as a husband then as Sam's father.

She shuts down the computer and, approaching the living room, hears talking.

"I want to learn how to snowboard," Sam says. "My friend Todd does, and he keeps asking me . . ."

"I've heard it's like waterskiing," Adrienne says.

Cass says, "Let's go. And while we're eating, you can tell us about Todd."

Inside Sal's Pizza, with rock music nearly shaking the walls, Adrienne shouts, "I'm not eating here."

Just then, a waiter wearing a red-checked bandana comes to take their order.

"Tonight's special is Italian sausage on a bun," he says, holding an order pad ready.

As Cass knows her sister hates both loud music and meat, she says, "Can you give us a minute?"

When he's gone, she says, "There's a vegetarian lasagna in the freezer. It'll take a while, but let's go home and eat."

"Can I stay here with my friends? We were going to a movie after, remember?"

"You've got money, right?"

"Two twenties."

"Take this too," Adrienne says and, while pushing some stray hair behind an ear with one hand, gives her niece another twenty. "Buy your friends some treats."

"Wow," Sam says. "Thank you," and she puts the bill in her wallet. "Please pick me up at 10:30 . . . after the movie."

Outside, snowflakes swirl, and as they get near the car, Adrienne says, "Remember the liquor store."

Back at the apartment, Adrienne searches the kitchen cupboards.

"Where are the glasses?" she asks.

"Right of the sink," Cass says.

"They only had a small bottle of Glenfiddich. I'll drink any scotch, but this is my favourite."

Cass nods while she knocks the frozen lasagne from its aluminum pan into a microwaveable casserole dish. She lightly defrosts the lasagna and puts it in the already warmed oven.

"I'm sure the LCBO in Sudbury has lots," Adrienne says.

Ignoring this remark, Cass says, "This'll take time to cook. We can spend it catching up."

"Or we can read a couple of the letters Aunt Margaret sent. You pour the coffee and I'll get them."

When Adrienne returns with what looks like a box of chocolates, she hands it to Cass, who goes into the living room and puts it on the coffee table. She then settles into a chair, with Adrienne opposite her. Once opened, Cass sees that it's filled with papers. The documents give off a faint pipe-tobacco smell and have the slightly yellowed look of archival material.

Cass remembers Aunt Margaret, her father's sister, but she's not sure why. Maybe Margaret sent her a wedding gift. Just thinking of her makes Cass uneasy. When she tries to recall anything about her father, his sister, or his parents, she can't. It's like she's drifting in deep space.

"Why did Margaret send them?" she asks.

"When she was packing to move to London, she decided it was time someone else looked after them. She thought I might be interested."

"Are you?"

"I feel sad when I read them. They make me think about Dad. Do you remember him?"

"I was little."

"The letters will help."

"The past doesn't really interest me. I'd choose teaching about how peer pressure affects the development of addictions over researching in archives any day."

Cass is surprised at how trying to remember her childhood makes her not only sad, but angry. These mixed feelings confuse her, like those she has when a weather report promises sun only to change, mid-day, to predicting rain.

She's feeling hungry, so she goes to the kitchen and opens the oven to check the lasagna. It's beginning to bubble.

Shutting the door, she turns to Adrienne, who's followed her, and says, "It'll take a few more minutes. Let's see if I can make a salad."

She finds a small head of lettuce in the crisper, cuts off its browning edges, and tears it into pieces in a bowl. Then she adds some slightly wrinkled cherry tomatoes, the only other salad item in the fridge, and hopes Adrienne won't notice their condition. Luckily, there's a little Italian dressing left in a bottle on the fridge's door. She puts it next to the salad on the table and returns to the living room with Adrienne behind her.

Once they're sitting again, Adrienne says, "One of the three letters I want you to read says Mom had a stillborn baby while Dad was at war."

"Interesting. She never told me that."

"This is the first one," says Adrienne, handing Cass a piece of yellowing stationary.

She recognizes her father's scrawl and tries to decipher it.

ROCCA SAN GIOVANNI 09–12-43
5th Field Ambulance
1st Can. Div.
R.C.A.M.C.

Dear Mother and Father,

Your letter, which came yesterday, was the quickest I've received at the front. More than nine months have passed, but your cable about Gloria's stillbirth has never come. She looked so forward to the baby, but now she's alone, and I'm still trying to deal with my sadness. I wonder what else I've missed.

Love, Alex

"I should tell you, I haven't finished reading the letters, but so far, these three stood out as important," says Adrienne. "Tell me what you think," and she hands the next letter to Cass.

"I'm confused," Cass says. "Was the letter he received the day before the first he'd heard of the stillbirth?"

"I told you," Adrienne says. "There are probably some other letters dealing with this baby, but I just haven't read them yet."

"If this is the first, then him writing that he was still trying to deal with his sadness was certainly an understatement. How could anyone get over that kind of news in a day? If I'd written that I'd lost the baby after I'd told Eric I was pregnant, he'd have been on the next plane home from wherever he was with the Red Cross. Even after he'd gone back, he'd have been writing how it was hard to get over the thought of our lost child. Of course," she adds, "I didn't lose Sam, and he loves spending time with her when he comes home. Do you think our father, despite being a psychiatrist, didn't feel things deeply?"

"Maybe being at war didn't allow him time for contemplation," Adrienne says. "But I remember him, before he became a drunk, as being interested in our lives. The first thing he'd ask when he got home from work was how our day at school went. And he'd listen when we talked and say things that showed he cared. But I also think there was a clinical, almost cold side to him that he rarely showed, which was the psychiatrist in him."

"Give me an example," says Cass, then thinks she sounds too much like a professor.

"You know," says Adrienne, smiling and nodding her head. "I remember a time when he was still well enough to come to the dinner table. He took a sip of water then mumbled something like, 'Got to stop drinking . . . brings me down . . . depression getting worse,' which sounded like he was talking to a patient."

"Maybe you should have been a psychiatrist instead of a financial wizard," says Cass, but Adrienne hands her another piece of U. of T. stationary and says, "Read this."

Nov. 10, 1940

Dear Mother and Father,

When I'm not at lectures, I'm studying or sleeping. I rarely have time to play the old piano that's here. They've added two hours per week of military medicine to our class load instead of physical training — to prepare us for active duty. I know others are suffering from this war, so I need to steel myself for whatever might be asked of me.

These days, all the students talk about are internships. I questioned Toronto General's Chief of Medicine after a lecture he gave to my class here. He advises interns to take a rotation, including four months medicine, four months surgery, two months urology, and two of gynaecology, before specialization. After that, I talked to my dean. He said with my grades I could probably get any internship I wanted. I hope to get one at Toronto General where I've heard Doctor Thomson helps interns get placements for their specialties when they're ready. My real interest is psychiatry, and Toronto General has that. As soldiers suffering from battle fatigue will be returning from the war, it's a field with a future. I know, Father, you think if I practice psychiatry, I'll be called a quack, and you're worried about how it will look to your friends. I'm surprised you don't want me to practice at London's psychiatric hospital when I get home. It would mean I could live there, and your grandchildren would be born in London.

For now, I have to get back to studying.

Love, Alex

"So he became a psychiatrist against his father's wishes," Cass says as she gets up from the dining room table.

"They were his wishes. Becoming a psychiatrist was one thing about his life that worked out."

"For a while. He used to be happy to see me when I snuck into his office. And later, when he just stared and didn't speak, he never stopped me from sitting with him."

"Did he ever smile or hug you, then?"

"Smile? Not that I remember," Cass says. "But I faintly recall him crying. Not exactly sobbing, but once I noticed water on his cheeks, and I asked him what was wrong."

"And?"

"He mumbled something about how he couldn't stop men from dying."

"Why do you think we each have such distinct memories of him, even though they happened years ago?" asks Adrienne.

"I don't know about you, but I loved being with him. Talking to him, while he still talked," says Cass.

"Me too," says Adrienne. "So, this note may interest you," and she hands Cass a small piece of lined paper, which, considering the date, was probably torn from one of the scribblers she remembers him using for his work.

1959

Mother,

You've always understood me. The girls are doing well. Today, I lost my battle-fatigue patients at the hospital, and we could use this money. It would help if Gloria could teach, but she can't. Married women aren't allowed in the classroom, as if their carnal knowledge might rub off on the children. Besides, if she could return to teaching, people would think I couldn't provide for my family. In order to do that now, I'll have to look for more patients in need of psychiatry.

When I'm alone in the den, I can't stop thinking about the dead. It's as if they're calling me to join them.

Alex

"Oh my," says Cass, as if searching for words. She pauses a long time and finally adds, "Those last two sentences could be interpreted in several ways, and even then, we can't know for sure what he meant."

"Tell me."

"The one time in his life he's experienced much death is WWII, and saving the dying would have been his priority during the war. He might be saying that he can't stop remembering all the soldiers who died while he was trying to save them, which made him feel guilty. And that would explain his next sentence. If he joined the men he couldn't save, then he wouldn't have to feel guilty anymore."

"Well, that would explain his tears that time," says Adrienne.

"There's another way, probably many ways, of reading this, too," Cass says. "He might not be able to forget the sight of mangled, dying men as they're brought to him from a battlefield. There'd have been lots of blood, blown off or mangled limbs, and a great deal of screaming. He'd have wanted to erase those sights, even as he attempted to stem the bleeding or clean blood from corpses. And if he joined the corpses, he wouldn't have to see those things again."

"Either interpretation is awful to contemplate," says Adrienne.

"So let's stop trying to figure it out. He was a psychiatrist by the time he wrote this note. I suspect he knew what he meant, and that's what matters," says Cass. "Anyway, the lasagna must be ready."

"Good," Adrienne says. "I'm hungry, so let's drop the seriousness. I've been meaning to say I like your hair. Those bronze highlights suit you. I bet both men and women find it attractive. My hair could use a tint and trim. I just haven't gotten around to it."

"There aren't any men other than colleagues, and if I were interested, Sam would complicate the relationship. I've certainly never wanted any gossip around town that she might hear. After all, I *am* still married. But what about you, any prospects?"

While she waits for the answer, Cass reminds herself that Sam's loyalty to Eric is the real reason she's avoided liaisons with North Bay men. She's carefully kept the few dalliances she's had at out-of-town conferences to herself.

"You mean romantic?" Adrienne asks. "Mom introduced me to a policeman. Retired, young, drops by to chat. I actually think she may be paying him to check on me. You know, to see if I'm okay."

"Where did she meet him?"

"John got him to help her break into my house."

"Why would she . . . ?"

"She claims she was afraid I'd do something foolish when I got downsized."

"Like what?"

"I'm not sure, but I've never seen her look as frightened as she did that day . . . As if she'd lost all her money on the stock market. Have you ever seen her look like that?"

"Probably, but I can't think of a time right now."

Cass would like to get back to talking about Adrienne's job loss. She knows her sister was fired but won't discuss it; she always finds a way to change the subject. Adrienne's own use of the word "downsized" reminds Cass of how their mother always whitewashed the truth, keeping their social status in mind. For Cass's grade twelve genealogy project, she discovered her father's family was Irish rather than Scottish and had emigrated, steerage class, during the potato famine. When she asked her mother about it, Gloria shrugged and said something about the errors in ships' records

and the spelling of names. Then she said again that she knew her husband's heritage was Scottish landed gentry.
While they're clearing the dinner dishes, Adrienne says, "You know, I'd like another drink."

"Let's have coffee instead. I don't want Sam to see you even slightly tipsy."

"I'll remember that."

Soon the aroma of coffee fills the kitchen. Adrienne sneezes loudly while Cass is getting down mugs, which makes her drop one on the counter. Thankfully, it doesn't break.

"You're a bit jumpy," Adrienne says. "I didn't mean to startle you."

"I know. Sudden, loud noises do that to me."

"Like a gunshot? I'll bet you were startled when Dad shot his handgun in his study. The bullet just missed hitting you."

"Mom always denied that happened, and I believe her. I can't imagine that I made him fire just by startling him while he was cleaning his gun. That's crazy!"

"I remember when it happened. You were screaming and didn't stop for a long time."

"It does sound weird that the gun was loaded while he was cleaning it," Adrienne says. "It can't be normal to do that."

"Normal? A loaded gun would be dangerous any time. It would be especially dangerous to clean it with children around," says Cass. "That's why I don't . . . I just can't believe. But listen, if there's something in his letters you think I should hear, call me." Then she pours milk into both mugs.

"I will. I'm glad to have them. They make me feel closer to him. But I'm having trouble, making myself read them. They make me sad, and I don't need more of that right now."

"You don't have to," Cass says. "What'll they teach you that you don't already know? He died and left Mom to manage on life insurance."

"It wasn't on purpose. One day, while you were in the kitchen having a snack, I came home from piano, and the ambulance had taken him away."

"I remember how Mom didn't like to talk about him. Now

that I think about it, her face used to look frightened when I asked, like what you said. As if she were lying or had a secret.

"Speaking of secrets, I know something about John." She tries hard not to look smug because she thinks she knows something that Adrienne doesn't. "He was interned in Camp Petawawa after Italy declared war on Britain. A lot of Italian-Canadians were."

"Interesting," Adrienne says and habitually tucks her loose hair back behind her ear. "He was talking about his war service the other day, but he didn't mention that. How did you know?"

"We talked on the phone in June 1994. The Normandy landing's Fiftieth Anniversary. He was emotional, said he couldn't watch it on TV. He never got over being interned and then conscripted."

"I can empathize with that," Adrienne says, "I'm sure the feelings around participating in any war are hard, but if you'd been interned and then had to take part . . . ."

Cass nods then looks at her watch. "It's time to get Sam."

"I'll put these back," Adrienne says and carries the chocolate box down the hall.

Cass stares at the table while wiping it with a dishcloth. She's baffled by the feeling of loss the letters give her. Her eyes focus on the deep-purple veins running along her fist. Her hand is like her mother's. Her life is like her mother's. A woman alone with her children. Cass decided not to follow Eric before she knew she was pregnant with Sam, choosing a career and small-city life rather than trailing him halfway across the world. Her mother had no choice. She was thrust by her husband's death into single parenthood.

Cass knows she sat on her father's lap in his den, but when she tries to recall more, that tiny memory of him, face wet, is all that comes to mind. Is she doomed to forget him entirely? Angry, she tosses the dishcloth into the sink and whispers to herself, "Erase him and his stupid letters. Put on your coat, pick up Sam, and get on with your life."

For three days, snow blankets the city like a white eiderdown. By midweek, Adrienne uses Cass's car to shop for much-needed groceries. Then she cooks dinner while Cass finishes her marking. She likes to hand back essays and exams as quickly as possible, because she knows students learn more from their mistakes by correcting them immediately. Once she's recorded the marks, she checks her email. To her surprise, there's one from Eric.

TO: Sam Swanson and Cass Muir
SUBJECT: Feeling Tired

Dear Sam and Cass,

I know the work I'm doing is important, but sometimes I feel, at forty-four, that I'm getting too old and tired to help people get their lives back together after disasters. It's just too emotionally exhausting for me. Maybe I'm having a mid-life crisis. All I can think about is my family. Send me a postcard, or better yet, email me.
Lots of love,
Dad

Despite the fact that he's worked in very remote places without email capabilities, Eric is now at the head-office in Switzerland, so he can send this message. She prints it out for Sam to read when she gets home. Who knows what he'll think or say next? When she's truthful, she admits her marriage to Eric, a loping, bespectacled man with a mop of wavy-blonde hair, has meant almost everything to her and Sam over the years. On the close-to-a-dozen times he's returned to Canada — for his sister's wedding, his mother's funeral, International Red Cross business, or because he missed Sam and Cass — they've met him in Ottawa or Toronto. They've stayed at hotels and acted like tourists, taking Sam to see dinosaurs at the museum, a children's play if there was one, and always Italian food, Sam's favourite.

Each trip, he and Cass have enthusiastically shared a bed, their lovemaking lasting most of the night. And she knows that both intellectually and sexually they're perfectly matched. She admires him, greatly, for his aid work, yet when he returns to it, she's left lonely and, except for the odd encounter at conferences, celibate again. Though intermittent, their sex-life has been remarkable, but she knows if she'd moved with him and never found satisfying work there, she'd have become dangerously depressed. Her work has been satisfying, helped keep boredom at bay, and paid the rent. If he ever moved back to Canada, she'd try to reconcile with him, but with conditions.

There are schools where she could teach in Vancouver or on Vancouver Island, but she knows, in all likelihood, this is *not* going to happen. To erase him from her mind, she gets to work. By the time Adrienne calls her for dinner, she's finished grading last Friday's pop-quizzes. Tomorrow, they'll go to Sudbury.

Cass pilots her car over the unlit road from Sudbury as Adrienne snores beside her. Sam had asked a friend to sleep over in case they were late getting home. As they were well on their way, she's not worried about the time, but the shopping trip itself is making her anxious.

On her way out of North Bay, Cass had used the bank's cash machine near the front door rather than lining up for a teller. Her account, still in the black after payday but before this month's automatic withdrawals, was too tempting. She took the balance. Now, instead of feeling good about her purchases, she'll have to scrimp and worry like she was unemployed, and she still won't be able to cover the month's bills. She always overspends, thinking the purchases will improve her image at the university, but when she has to pay the automatic withdrawals, she gets depressed.

She turns on the radio, lowering the volume so Adrienne can sleep. CBC is into evening programming, and the announcer's voice soothes her, so she concentrates on the road. Fifteen minutes out of Sudbury, she notices again how this long stretch of highway is unlit. Except for the glow of her car's headlights, total darkness envelopes her. Farmland on either side of the road is cloaked in gloom. Then, the lights from the first Highway 17 town, Coniston, appear. As each village emerges from obscurity — Wahnapitae, Markstay, Hagar, Warren, and Verner — she's relieved to be driving home. Beyond Sturgeon Falls she sees, through the side window, countless stars lighting the sky. She's about to wake Adrienne to show her when CBC radio's long dash signals the hour.

Hearing this, Adrienne stirs, and Cass says, "Look to your right. The stars."

Adrienne rubs her eyes, then turns her head and says, "Wow. There's too much light in Toronto to see this many. Pull over so I can look."

Cass finds a widened shoulder, probably a farmer's driveway, and steers onto the gravel there. With her four-ways flashing, she turns off the car and they get out.

"Now, give me an astronomy lesson."

"We're facing east," Adrienne says. "To the left, you can see the Dippers. You know, Ursa Major and Ursa Minor."

"Even I recognize them."

"Straight ahead are Gemini, then Cancer and Leo. They don't look like their names."

"You mean like twins or a lion?"

"You do know this."

"Fragments," Cass says. "Like anyone who's ever gone camping." They get back into the car, and she steers it onto the highway. "How did you get so interested?"

"On a trip to London to visit his parents, Daddy took us out in the country near Ingersoll. We looked at the stars. The night was so clear, it seemed like Orion and his belt came down to meet us. I've never forgotten."

"How old were you?"

"Nine," Adrienne says and tucks her hair behind her ears.

"That would make me six. I want to remember, but I can't."

"I wish you could, too," Adrienne says and rubs Cass's shoulder affectionately. "Because soon after, he stopped wanting to look at the stars."

As Adrienne rarely shows overt affection, Cass forces herself to focus on the road so she won't cry. She starts seeing North Bay hotels advertised on billboards, and soon Adrienne falls back to sleep. In the car's dark silence, Cass recalls the smell of pipe tobacco from when she sat on her father's lap. She wears a navy, smocked dress, with a collar she can still feel choking her. He recites the title of her chosen book, *The Boxcar Children*, and begins to read. The book, with the inscription, *Love Daddy* and *Happy Birthday Cassie, July 12, 1958*, still sits on her bookshelf. Nestled in her father's arms, she feels secure.

August 12, 1943

60 Edmonton casualties yesterday from Leonforte — 20 dead and the rest injured — didn't get them because nearest car post only 3½ miles on foot, and we're farther than that for stretcher bearers to carry injured.

Cpl. Joe Johnson, Grant's friend from Edmonton, was hit by a Jerry tank, killed — comrades recognized curly red hair on skull — Grant still catatonic after hearing news — though I try, can't reach him.

Matthew, young man with stitched balls, is favourite of one nurse — hope she works her magic on his equipment. Though I'm not injured, my favourite nurse is Velma Miles — hope I'm her favourite doctor.

Americans are rumoured as Regalbuto bombers — 30 dead or injured — we don't mention it. Canadians took mules from near Agira for carrying wounded — mules go where jeeps can't — fierce fighting in interior — Canadians beat Panzer Grenadiers 1st Parachute Division with help from air.

Heard Mussolini overthrown, replaced by Badoglio — not considered fascist — when heard there was wild cheering in mess tent — men planned party for tonight if we can find women for dancing. I've asked Velma — after hearing this news, men feel good, think fighting in Sicily soon finished — next we'll cross to mainland by boat and fight all the way to Rome.

FOUR

Adrienne

While unpacking the next morning, Adrienne thinks about how useful she'd felt at Cass's. Although she's given catered parties since Graham left seven years ago, she hasn't cooked anything for anyone. The apartment she and Graham first rented, years ago, had sloping floors, crooked doorways, and rummage-sale furniture. While she wanted an upscale lifestyle even then, she'd still hurry home from work and run the vacuum while dinner cooked. Then she'd change into something alluring as a signal she felt like sex, even if she didn't. She so hoped for a baby that she converted the upstairs den to a nursery. She never got pregnant, but now she sees her childlessness as a blessing. She doesn't have to divide her time and energy between mothering and working, and she's never wanted to bring up a child alone, like Cass has. Besides, Graham was too self-involved to be a good father.

She slides the new jeans she bought in Sudbury over other pants and jams the sweatshirts into her dresser, knowing she doesn't need them. Finally, she returns the pile of letters she'd taken to North Bay to her desk and stops there a moment to examine its contents. Her paternal grandmother had inscribed the pictures' backs in block capitals, and Margaret's handwriting is under the inscriptions.

Impulsively, she decides to put the photos and letters in date order, for methodical reading. She takes the box downstairs and uses the dining-room table to sort its contents. She looks again at the three letters she'd taken to show Cass, which are at the top of the pile, and integrates them by date. Three rows of papers and photos soon cover the table's surface. She begins examining them and thinks she might copy the most interesting items to make a scrapbook for Cass. Then, when her sister sees them framed in complimentary colours and laid out attractively, she might change her mind about archival material. After all, Cass had been willing to talk about what the letters possibly meant, after she'd read them.

In the first photo, a woman holds a baby.
PICNIC AT INGERSOLL, SEPTEMBER, 1917
Baby Alex and your grandmother on an outing with friends. Her clothes were always the newest fashion.

The mention of Grandma Muir's fashionable clothes makes Adrienne wonder if that's where she got her love of dressing well.

A child stands on the porch of a house, holding a rifle.
ALEX AT HILLVIEW, 1919
Alex loved his toy rifle and learned to hunt early. Father hunted at the London Hunt Club, but Grandpa shot ducks in the country.

Adrienne thinks her father was too young to love guns.

A boy sits on a swing while a woman holds its chains.
DOMINION DAY, 1926
Aunt Muriel, Father's sister, swings Alex at Hillview. She married Dr. Brendan O'Donnell, an Irish-Catholic, who gave Alex his first taste of wine and started him drinking.

An image of her father in his den, drinking, makes Adrienne wish he'd never met Dr. O'Donnell. She considers, only briefly, whether her own fondness for alcohol is related to his. To accept this about herself would mean remembering the pain his drinking inflicted on her family. In particular, she remembers how, after he'd sat all day in his den drinking scotch, when he finally got to the dinner table, he couldn't converse. By then, he was incapable of showing any interest in his daughters or his wife, which he'd done prior to drinking alcohol so heavily. Her mind turns again to her own habit and how that might affect any family she hopes to have. Because having children is almost impossible at this stage in her life, she dismisses that thought as irrelevant.

A boy and a girl stand on a lawn where hollyhocks shade the house's porch.
MARGARET AND ALEX AT HILLVIEW, 1927
Alex and I, not dressed for the farm, often went to Grandma and Grandpa Muir's: he in knickers, me in dresses.

Alex and Aunt Margaret sit on lawn chairs in front of Hillview.
BACK TO SCHOOL, 1931
During the depression, we summered at the farm because food was in good supply there. Mother and Father couldn't afford to pay as many staff for their stores then, so they worked more.

Adrienne is thrilled to see these pictures of her father as a child. He appears well dressed and cared for, and he looks happy, which she saw less and less in him while he was still alive. She intends to keep reading the letters, hoping she'll find other instances of him enjoying life.

The next dates are on letters: the first on lined paper torn from a notebook, like the paper where the note saying, "I can't stop thinking about the dead," is written.

Toronto, 1938

Dear Margaret,

Thank you for loaning me the money so I could pay off my gambling debts. Please don't tell our parents how much I needed; they'll stop sending money. As soon as I get ahead, I'll try to pay you back.
Love, Alex

Adrienne never knew her father as a gambler, but that doesn't mean he wasn't, which might have caused problems in her parents' marriage.

University of Toronto
January 10, 1939

Dear Mother and Father,

Thank you for the cigarette case you sent for New Year's. My friends say it's sophisticated. We had a smashing time at the Chateau Laurier that night; I escorted George's sister, who's Margaret's age. She's beautiful, but she's not fun like Gloria. You're right! I need to socialize with my classmates. Knowing them might prove useful to my career.

Gloria likes living with Grandma and Grandpa Muir and teaching Latin. They don't charge her board, and their hired man drives her to school and picks her up. The MacLeans know Gloria is chaperoned, and although they're Presbyterian, they're happy she at least attends church.

Love, Alex

Although this letter doesn't reveal anything particular about her father's beliefs, it confirms that his family attended an Anglican church. She remembers her mother confirming this detail when, after her father died, she inferred that Anglicans considered themselves socially superior to Presbyterians, at least in London.

Toronto, April 8, 1941

Dear Mother,

Just a note to wish you Happy Birthday. There's something in the mail from Birks, which is still the swankiest store in Toronto. I want you and Father to bring Gloria to my graduation. I'll soon be off to war, so in case I don't come back, we should celebrate while we have the chance.

Love, Alex

Adrienne thinks that her father's shopping at Birks, which has always been expensive, could be an indication of his inability to look after money. He could have sent his mother a card or even candy.

She reads the next letter, which mentions her parents' engagement, and sets it aside to show her mother, along with the three letters she'd shown Cass. The emphasis this one places on her mother's family attending the Presbyterian Church "every Sunday" surprises her. She doesn't know anyone who attends church anymore, except maybe at Christmas or Easter, and even those people are rare. It's amazing to her how social mores have changed in the fifty-plus years since it was written.

Toronto General Hospital
June 18, 1941

Dear Mother and Father,

I've half a mind to ignore your last letter's comment about Gloria not fitting in with our family. Mr. MacLean may not have as much money as you, but his father was a teacher in Scotland, and he himself is a pharmacist. He and his wife play musical instruments, and although they go to a Presbyterian church and you are Anglican, they go every Sunday. So you see, Gloria comes from a good family.

I must go as the nurses are calling me to sedate a soldier whose been discharged back to Canada for special psychiatric treatment. He saw his friend shot and killed in battle over there, and he's keeping the whole ward up with his frenzied shouting.

Love, Alex

The soldier who's described here reminds her of what Cass speculated their father meant when he said the dead were calling him to join them.

The next item is another photograph.

Two young women stand outside near an older woman, where a table is set for a meal.
DOMINION DAY, HILLVIEW, 1941
Gloria and me, with Aunt Muriel, at the last Dominion Day picnic. After the war started, it was hard to get sugar for cake and ice cream.

Toronto General Hospital
July 25, 1941

My dearest Mother and Father,

I'm doing my internship at this hospital, which is known for psychiatric public service. After our internships, those who want can go on active duty.

Since coming here, I've done minor surgeries like bone-setting, tonsillectomies, and "female problem" operations, which I won't name. I'm good at surgery, but neuroses interest me more, and sometimes we see prominent people with such problems. Here we link neurology and psychiatry and sedate for rest and rehabilitation, although I'm sure psychiatric hospitals treat neuroses differently. As we can't admit patients indefinitely, psychiatrists can't talk at length to patients, so we don't utilize Freud's theories or methods.

Another intern invited me to the Rosedale Golf Club, very upper-crust, for three weekends from now, so please send me extra money for new golf shoes.
Love, Alex

Adrienne notes this as her father's first mention of his interest in psychiatry, which is obviously more important to him than surgery. As he asks for extra money for new golf shoes, she wonders if his old shoes are really worn out or whether he wants new shoes to impress his colleagues with his family's wealth. She puts another letter, dated October 4, 1941, aside in a growing pile to show her mother. Although she hadn't planned on spending the day this way, examining her father's memorabilia is like eating potato chips. Now that she's eaten one, they're addictive. Reading them is as compelling as reading a thriller, and they've given her a window into a part of her father's life about which she'd previously known nothing.

Toronto General Hospital
October 21, 1941

Dear Mother and Father,

It was good to see you at Thanksgiving. As you and Grandpa Muir share my allowance, please send it by the first of each month. I can't believe you've cut it because I receive army pay.
Alex

Again, Adrienne wonders why her father asks for money so often. Does a man studying to be a doctor really have enough time on his hands to spend that much?

Toronto General Hospital
January 23, 1942

Dear Mother and Father,

Thanks for bringing Gloria here for Christmas. I was horrified when, during dinner, you said, "This is the wrong time for you to get engaged." I intend to marry Gloria. We won't wait any longer than necessary and especially not until after the war. If the army will let me off, we hope to marry on Dominion Day. If we don't, I may be shipped out then killed, and we won't have even a few days to experience wedded bliss.
Love, A.

On reading this, Adrienne sees it as more evidence her paternal grandparents were reluctant for her parents to marry.

The next item is another photo.

A woman in floor-length, white satin and a uniformed man stand under a rose-covered arbour, facing each other and smiling.
ALEX'S WEDDING, HILLVIEW, July 1, 1942

Your parent's wedding. They seemed happy, as they couldn't stop smiling, and they kept kissing each other. It was like a Dominion Day picnic. Mother spared no expense. I was maid-of-honour, as many of Gloria's friends had already accompanied their husbands to military camps before being shipped out.

Adrienne is happy that her father overcame his parents' objections to his marrying her mother. After all, neither she nor Cass would exist without their parents' love.

ENGLAND September 28, 1942
C.G.R.U.
R.C.A.M.C.

My dearest Mother and Father,

The weather is cold and damp, yet our quarters won't have fires for a month. German propaganda is on the radio, and planes come and go all day. I can only imagine the bombs they drop at their destination. Grandma and Grandpa Muir sent me snapshots of Gloria. They miss her at Hillview, and she misses them and her teaching, which, as a married woman, she can't do. My cases include head colds, stomach flu, and toothaches. I, like her, am bored. A few tonsillitis or appendicitis cases would help. The meals are good. At night we play bridge and have a few drinks. The best thing about being in the middle of a war is that, despite missing Gloria, I'm enjoying the company of men.
A.

This reminds Adrienne how, before drinking took over his life, her parents used to invite friends, usually other doctors and their wives, to play bridge on a Saturday night. Her father would serve drinks, and her mother would make sandwiches and cakes for a midnight snack. Her father would usually win. Now that she thinks of it, before her parents woke the next morning, she'd see money was left on the card table. Because of the letter that mentions his gambling, she wonders if the bills were his winnings from betting.

ENGLAND October 25, 1942
C.G.R.U.
R.C.A.M.C.

Dear Mother and Father,

I'm back from my amputations course in Edinburgh. Even with heat, I'm cold in this bloody place. After the course was finished, I took a few days leave and visited Gloria's great aunt and uncle. They live quite close to where the course was held in Edinburgh. They liked my Canadian stories and treated me like family. Despite shortages, we kept eating. What with elevenses and high tea, including a silver service and fine china like we have at home, I'll have to lose a few pounds. My uniform is getting tight, and I'm still awaiting posting.
Love, Alex

To Adrienne, this letter shows that because her father used his precious leave to visit her mother's Scottish relatives, he wanted to please her. She wonders whether any of them are still alive, and if they are and she visited them, they might tell her their impressions of what her father felt about being at war.

ENGLAND December 27, 1942
C.G.R.U.
R.C.M.A.C.

Dear Mother and Father,

It doesn't feel like Christmas in the blackout. Thank you for the sweater. I've written thanking Grandma and Grandpa for pyjamas and the money they wired, Aunt Muriel for handkerchiefs, and Gloria for mittens. She's saving the small amount of money I'm able to send to get an apartment. Margaret writes that she likes library work, but her social life is almost non-existent. All of her men friends are overseas.
Love, Alex

For a moment, Adrienne wonders why her father kept so much money for himself rather than sending her mother more for an apartment.

ENGLAND April 2, 1943
#15 G.H.
R.C.A.M.C.

Dear Mother and Father,

Tomorrow, Gloria is due. Please wire me the moment the baby is born. She should keep staying at her parents' in London and not live in her apartment until she can manage alone at night. I miss her terribly and look forward to hearing about our baby's birth. I'm treating soldiers, recently arrived from Canada, for diphtheria. I'm not sure whether this disease has reached London yet, but Gloria's parents, the MacLeans, should arrange for their whole household to be immunized, so neither Gloria nor the baby catches it. You, and everyone else in London for that matter, should be immunized for when you first see your grandchild. Do what you can to get me news about the birth.

Next week, I'm in a golf tournament between officers, NCOs, and other ranks, which should be fun. We've set up a betting pool, so if I do well, I might make a little money. Playing helps me to forget the waiting, just as playing the piano does.

Invite the MacLeans for Sunday dinner with Gloria and Grandma and Grandpa Muir. After all, my in-laws just live a few blocks from you in London. Gloria writes that she barely sees you, and once the baby is born, you'll be grandparents and want to be included. Don't make her parents feel snubbed.

Love, Alex

Playing golf in the middle of a war seems a necessary distraction to Adrienne, but playing for money is also an example of him liking to gamble. Maybe that explains why he didn't send more money to her mother. He'd gambled any extra away.

NAPLES October 11, 1943

Dear Mother and Father,

We were holed up in the wet when several MOs got leave and came here where it's warmer. My friend, Grant Chapman, is here too. Smoke is pouring from Mount Vesuvius, which is ready to erupt.

All of the women in this city, from girls to great-grandmothers, are welcoming. They hug us and love to cook for us. It's odd that a battle-worn, rubble-strewn place could feel like home. Though people here are hungry, the meals at inns are respectable: dishes with tomatoes, a little seafood, and various beans. Who knows where they get the makings.

An officer with money can buy anything here. I am learning to speak Italian, and I've bought things like Venetian glass, which I'll send home labelled "Officer's Kit Surplus". The Luger pistol and case are for me. The censors here said there'd be no problem with shipping them. The African mahogany pipes are for you, Father, now that you can't get cigars from Grandpa Semple's factory, which you wrote that Mother sold. Give the glass, small statue, and jewelry to Gloria. Since our baby's stillbirth was six months ago, I would think she has adjusted to being childless. If not, I hope these gifts will cheer her. I do so wish I could be there myself to comfort her.

Love, Alex

On reading this, Adrienne thinks, rather than buying himself a gun, he could have sent what it cost to her mother. But she remembers how Gloria loved the beautiful blue Venetian glasses, decorated with gold scrolling around their bottoms and used only for tomato juice at Christmas. Then there were the pipes, sitting in a row on a shelf in her grandfather's basement room. He called it his smoking room, where no one else was allowed unless invited. She also recalls a small case in her father's desk drawer with a key in the lock, a red ribbon hanging from it, which he said should never be opened. Maybe it contained his gun.

Although there are still unread letters, Adrienne puts them aside with the ones to show her mother. She needs time to digest the few she's read. Obviously, her parents' marriage had rocky patches.

Adrienne can't imagine going through the pain of childbirth only to find that the long-awaited baby was dead. As she'd promised to inform Cass of any interesting information she gleaned from the letters, she begins to dial her sister's number. Halfway through, she stops. Cass won't be interested in this news, and if Adrienne calls her mother, she knows Gloria will refuse to discuss the past.

She thinks of Sonia, an adopted woman in her astronomy club who spent months searching for her birth parents. She wrote hospitals, churches, and doctors. With every piece of new information, she scoured newspaper archives only to discover her mother was dead and her father was in prison. She was so shocked that she couldn't bring herself to contact her father. By comparison, Adrienne's own father was in his den drinking and, while dinner cooked, died. This was hardly a reason for his family to refuse to talk about him after his death.

When she was a girl in the '50s, she'd watch out the living room window for her father to come home. He'd walk from the subway after work, his clothes smelling of the hospital and pipe tobacco. If his mood were good, he'd tousle her hair and hug her when he came through the door. Once, he'd hung up his coat and gone to the record player. From his paper-sleeved 78s, he'd chosen a swing tune and placed it on the turntable, then pulled her mother from the steaming kitchen into their front room.

"They've put me in charge of battle-fatigue patients," he'd said. "We'll have more money. Let's buy a cottage."

They danced, swaying and twirling, until they collapsed on the couch. He played the living-room piano until late that evening. After the dishes, he and her mother sang along to "Don't Sit Under the Apple Tree", "Chattanooga Choo Choo", and "We'll Meet Again" while Adrienne and Cass drifted into sleep.

She remembers her father reading to her, when she was younger, before she nodded off. After she could read, he steered her toward his boyhood favourites: Jules Verne's classic, *Twenty Thousand Leagues Under the Sea*, or C. F. Forester's swashbuckling tales. Because she didn't warm to his taste, he listened while she talked about her favourites: *The Secret Garden* or *Anne of Avonlea*. But as time passed, these special times when she heard her parents singing, or she and her father talked about books, happened less as he spent more time in his den, and then they stopped.

Adrienne's watch says she's been staring out the window at the streetlamp for twelve minutes. Chilled by a draft, she reaches for the sweater on her chair's back. She should call a handyman to caulk the frame or install a new window. If her father were alive now, maybe he'd be retired and like to fill his time doing repair jobs around her house. But she doesn't know much about him. Her mother never talked about his student days or whether he liked sports, though she knows he and her mother played golf. Did he join the debate team? Are his war buddies still alive? Did his hospital colleagues like him? She knows her mother won't answer these questions. If they were alive, she could try to find them and talk to his school friends or his military chums. That way, she might get information about him even her mother doesn't know.

She checks her phone messages and deletes the invitations from two former co-workers to have lunch. Adrienne suspects they only want information that would help their own careers. Her ex-assistant, Jessica, wants to know what to tell her previous clients about her departure. Dell, from her astronomy club, called about next week's meeting. John and her mother heard she had fun in North Bay and will call next week. The retired cop, Tony, wants to share a pizza after he finishes jogging.

It's 7:00 p.m. Tony's message came after John's, so he must mean *now*. Friday night. He's never phoned her before, and they've never eaten together. All they've ever done is talk on her steps when he's finished running. They talk about her lost job, how astronomy interests her, or how he burned out on police work and started his own security firm. Not only is he good looking, but she likes him because he listens to her and responds with attention, though he may only be pretending. Yet she's never seen any indication of that.

When she thinks of the trustworthy feeling she gets from him compared to how she felt about Graham at the end, there's no resemblance. As soon as Graham saw that Adrienne was better at sales, he began to lie about his success. He could have continued, without consequences, except one month he left the firm's statement out on his desk. As she passed, she saw how he hadn't made a cent in the last thirty days. When she mentioned it to him, he claimed it was an entry error by the finance department, but the way he looked away when he said it told her he was lying. She never trusted him again.

In contrast, Tony never hesitates to look straight into her eyes when he speaks, so she believes she can trust him, even when they're alone. After all, he's never even gotten close enough to touch her. Besides, he's the first man since Graham who makes her feel like her heart is in her throat when she's near him. She tells herself not to get too attached, so then she won't get hurt. After all, maybe these visits are only because John hired him to break in. Maybe his heart doesn't do anything when she's near. Maybe, as a pro, Tony's just following up.

The doorbell rings. In the bathroom, she's appalled by her unkempt hair, but she applies a swipe of the nearest lipstick, goes downstairs, and opens the door. It's him, fashionable in jeans and a leather jacket instead of his standard sweatpants.

"Did you get my message?"

"I thought you'd stop on your way home from jogging."

"I needed a shower. Let's walk to the corner, grab a bite, and I'll walk you back."

Adrienne considers changing, after all it's their first date, but instead, he sits on the front stoop while she combs her hair and applies makeup. Then, she puts the mail that's collected in the box onto the hall table, and they set out for an Italian restaurant he knows on St. Clair.

"Have you been away?" he asks, to start the conversation.

"To my sister's in North Bay. Why?"

"The mailbox was stuffed, a dangerous sign to thieves. I rang the doorbell, but no answer."

"It snowed for three days, so we stayed home, watched movies, and read my father's letters from the war. Then we went to Sudbury to shop."

"I was born in Sudbury. My mother still lives there."

"Why did you leave?" After she's asked, she thinks the question's too personal, but he surprises her and answers, which means he won't hide things from her.

"I wanted to be a policeman, but Sudbury wasn't the place to learn, so I left."

She wants to know more but thinks probing would be rude, so she doesn't ask why.

Instead, she says, "We must be here. The air smells like freshly-baked pizza."

He opens the door, and she's deafened by loud voices and hearty laughter. Seeing the other patrons dressed in jeans and sweatshirts, she's glad she didn't change. As there's no one offering to seat them, Tony indicates a table in an alcove to his right.

He holds out a chair for her and says, "It's quieter here, or rather, not quite as noisy. We might be able to hear each other talk."

"I'd like that," she says, and smiles. "We'll split the bill. Should we start with a litre of red?"

"Not for me, thanks."

"Are you afraid to tell my mother we were drinking?" she asks, then is glad when he laughs.

"I ran today. Water is what I need."

"Did John hire you to watch me while they're in Florida?" she asks, half seriously.

"He knew you'd pull yourself together — the job didn't have long-term prospects. But I like taking a break from running to talk to you."

"I like that, too," Adrienne says, feeling her heart constrict her breathing.

A man in a starched white jacket and apron over black pants approaches to take their orders. They decide to share a medium Margherita pizza and a chef's salad.

"I remember when I first went to Italy," says Adrienne. "I'd been planning on trying every type of pizza available while there, but I soon discovered this was the most popular."

"Legend says pizza originated in Naples," says Tony. "It's in a poor region of Italy, and this pizza only needs flour, yeast, and water for the crust and tomatoes, basil, and buffalo mozzarella cheese for the top, all easily available there."

"You seem quite versed on this topic. Did your ancestors come from Naples?"

"Yes. And when I was growing up, my grandmother, who was born there, used to talk about the terrible poverty and crime that made her want to come to Canada."

"I'll bet those stories influenced you to become a policeman."

"Probably," he says, "and some other things, too. But tell me, have you been to Italy often?"

"Only once after that. My firm went on a fundraising bus tour with some of our wealthiest clients. It wasn't just Italy. We went to several countries. It took three weeks. It was great fun seeing so much of Europe, but after three weeks I'd had enough."

"But it sounds like you like travelling."

"For sure. And now I'll probably have more time to do it."

"Where would you like to go?"

"The next place I want to go is the UK: England, Scotland, Ireland, and Wales. My ancestors come from there, mostly Scotland and Ireland, and I wouldn't mind finding out whether any of them are still alive and visiting them if they are."

Adrienne decides not to tell him that she's already been to parts of the UK on the fundraising tour because Graham and she went together. He spent the whole tour bragging to the young women, both married and unmarried, about how successful he'd been in the investment business. Then, soon after that, she discovered how he'd lied to her about his earnings.

During that tour, the subject of where the money raised would go came up several times. As always, the CEO of the firm wanted to give it to small businesses that wanted to grow, and she wanted to invest it in the unemployed or underemployed who wanted to start new businesses. In particular, she'd like it to focus on women. She remembers, as she's waiting for Tony to continue talking, how angry the CEO had become at her voicing opposition to the firm's plan. After that, he never spoke pleasantly to her again but, rather, treated her with silence, or if he talked, it was in a blunt, cold voice. Now that she remembers his abruptness, she thinks her opposition to his plans was probably the main reason for her dismissal.

Finally, Tony's voice breaks her concentration, "I'd love to see those places, too. What would you think of travelling together?"

Adrienne feels almost dizzy contemplating that idea, but, thankfully, she's no longer afraid to get too involved with him, in case he hurts her. She's almost about to tell him that she'd take a trip with him when their waiter brings the drinks and says, "Your food is on the way."

"Good," she says, to no one in particular. "I'm hungry."

"Even if it's only pizza?" asks Tony.

"Are you kidding? It's one of my favourite foods. And I want to compare theirs to the ones from my favourite delivery-only place."

"If you say so," and Tony uses his napkin to cover the tomato stain on the white tablecloth where they're sitting. "Next time, we'll do some fine dining."

Walking back, she's cold and wishes she'd worn a scarf. She moves closer to him, and he hugs her shoulder.

"So chivalry is not dead," she says flippantly. "I'm much warmer now."

She puts her arm around his waist and breathes his soapy smell, then thinks about how walking with him now only happened because she lost her job.

"If you didn't like the snow in North Bay, you should visit your parents in Florida," he says, interrupting her thoughts.

"Mother and stepfather. My real father died of a heart attack . . . or so the story goes."

"What work did he do?"

"He was a GP, a doctor during the Italian campaign. After the war, he specialized in psychiatry," she says, but her mind wanders to being thankful that she's met and connected with Tony. And she already knows from reading the letters that losing her job has given her the chance to reconnect with her father, even if it's only to remember that he liked playing the piano and excelled in bridge and golfing. Soon, she'll go to the library downtown to research The

Italian Campaign of WWII, so the letters' locations make sense.

With that thought in mind, Adrienne feels Tony tighten his hug on her shoulder. All the way back from the restaurant, her mind's been drifting, but with this gesture, she consciously adjusts to his pace, and they begin to walk like hiking partners.

"Tell me more about your work," she says as they cross Bathurst and turn right.

"My business helps people keep burglars out or provides guards to corporations. That's how I know you shouldn't let your mail collect."

"If I go away again, I'll get someone to empty the box."

The frozen slush on the sidewalk down the block from her house makes walking treacherous.

"Aren't you glad I shovelled your walk while this was soft?" he asks, and she nods.

On the porch, she holds her keys up to her face and wishes she'd left on the light. Tony's arm slips from her back and he holds a miniature flashlight above her head, so her hands are encircled in light.

"I keep one in every coat."

She laughs and puts the key in the lock. His light sweeps toward her mailbox.

"See how much better that looks. Sorry, I do that sometimes. Lecture, I mean . . . But people don't realize what can happen."

"Thanks for the concern," she says, and, in the flashlight's glow, sees tenderness in his eyes. "And for a delicious dinner. Now I know where to get my pizza."

He smiles, and she notices his teeth: white, straight, and even. Another one of his attractive features. She doesn't want to invite him in or for him to feel forced to ask her out again, so she says, "Stop by when you're running."

"I will. And let's do dinner and a movie sometime soon."

"Sounds good to me."

He puts his hand on her shoulder and leans forward in the doorway until their lips touch. His mouth is soft and generous.

"See you soon," he says and walks down the steps.

She hangs up her coat and leans, for a minute, on the wall in the hallway, thinking about how much he excites her. She likes how this relationship is going. Slowly. So she's not apt to make mistakes. Although resting against the wall like a dreamy teenager reminds her of her youth, she knows she has to tackle the mail. Today, at the airport's bank machine, she discovered her chequing account was overdrawn by four thousand dollars. Her monthly automatic withdrawals for Toronto property taxes, utility payments, and RRSP payments are taken out of the bank account regardless of whether there's money in it. She knows that whether she gets a job or not, she has to get her life in order.

She'd noticed the sky clearing while walking home from dinner. Even with Toronto's light haze, she could go upstairs and search for stars. When she gazes through her telescope, she can almost feel the comfort of her father's arm around her in that London field. The mail can wait. It's not as if it hasn't waited six weeks already.

Upstairs, she rummages for her logbook. The last sighting she'd marked was New Year's Eve when she tried to find the Quadrantids meteor shower near Draco. She'd made time to search for this seasonal show, without luck, before a colleague's dinner party. She wonders now how many of her co-workers at that party knew she'd be getting the sack.

She gropes in the dark for the telescope and recalls how she and Cass stopped on the highway to look at the heavens. After turning on the table lamp, she counts back to that date, then marks it in her log as a naked-eye sighting. She has to tell the club something. Returning to her telescope, she looks for the North Star and laughs at her rudimentary astronomy skills, which, even in a sky blurred with light, are still reliable. Although Polaris is barely visible, she draws an imaginary line from it to where she knows Orion stands with three bright stars marking his belt. On his right shoulder is Betelgeuse, a red-variable supergiant. Diagonally opposite and marking his upraised left foot is Rigel, a blue-white supergiant double. Miraculously, she sees both. Here are winter's most magnificent stars, some of her father's favourites.

Long ago, when they couldn't agree on a book to read, he'd

recite these constellations. Now, with zero visibility, her telescope goes to where she knows Orion's belt stars are. Halfway down his sword's blade is M42, the Great Nebula, a barely visible mass of glowing gas. Buoyed by remembering its location, she looks for but doesn't find the open cluster, M35, in Gemini, near Castor's left foot. She's so frustrated by how the urban light pollution obliterates the stars that she creeps along the wall in the dark and goes downstairs to the mail. The descent is so slow that her mind wanders to how her father began to show disinterest in the constellations, his lifelong passion. Finally, when he would sit in the den, motionless except for lifting his liquor glass to his mouth, he had not spoken of the stars in years.

She carries her recent, unopened mail to the dining room and puts them next to her father's letters, along with an envelope from work the day she was let go. They've gone untouched all of this time. On opening them, she finds her income tax receipts, which remind her the filing date is coming soon. She'll start organizing the papers tomorrow.

Later, she wakes with her cheek resting on the table. After turning off the downstairs lights, she starts upstairs then goes back down and leaves the porch light on — for Tony.

September 6, 1943

Amidst aircraft fire we made an assault landing across Strait of Messina. Jerries dive-bombed beach — looking up saw enemy pilots in cockpits like allied pilots — hard to hate men like us.

Carleton and Yorks took Reggio — Italian troops rushed down mountains, surrendered — weather's warm here, but not dry like Sicily — when non-medical officers out of sight, we strip off shirts, get tanned — try not to feel jealous that Grant's more muscular . . .

Up mountains, Jerries blew bridges behind their troops war becoming serious — more and more dangerous to be here — our vehicles stopped so Engineers could repair crossings — MacPhee so smart he got engineering degree before medicine — he helped, so we must keep him alive.

Troops wet and cold — brawniest stretcher bearers, Ralph and Roger Quinn, lumberjacks from northern Ontario, sick with jaundice/hepatitis from contaminated water — evacuated quickly but new stretcher bearers not strong like Ralph or Roger, hope none of the injured is too heavy.

5th Field ordered north by main road — Jerries didn't blow bridges there. Moving to children's hospital — we'll be dry — a simple pleasure. No mail for weeks — Gloria's alone at home after months getting ready for baby — wish I could see her.

FIVE

Adrienne

Adrienne finds a cheque in-lieu-of-notice and another for severance pay in the sorted mail. She realizes this money will give her enough cash to cover her overdraft at the bank and add to her Registered Retirement Savings Plan. As long as she invests, she'll get income tax back and can live until November without touching her savings.

Although she'd deleted yesterday's messages, she remembers to phone Dell. He wants her to bring refreshments to this week's meeting now that she's not working and has time. She's shocked that he knows about her dismissal, but agrees to bring food. While wondering who else knows, she writes *recipes*, *shopping*, and *cooking* in her daybook.

Talking to Dell makes her think, again, about why she was fired. Although her CEO didn't give her a reason, and she was trying not to cry so she didn't ask, she can only think it might be because she'd disagreed with him on the firm's charity work. It could also be, and this is more likely, that her sales had shrunk for several years running, and she hadn't worked to improve them. She could hire a lawyer and fight the layoff, but she's not sure she wants to use her energy or money that way.

She's still in the kitchen when the doorbell startles her. Peeking through the front window, she can see Tony leaning against the railing. She opens the door, and he stands up straight.

"You've moved your mail," he says, looking at the hall table.

"I sorted it all weekend," she says and wishes she'd had her hair done or at least put on some makeup this morning.

"Come to the movies with me Friday night?"

"Can't! I have astronomy club, but I could go Saturday."

"Great. My treat."

"I prefer dutch. But we can negotiate. Call me later in the week to arrange a time?"

"I will. By the way, I just added to my RRSP. I probably should have talked to you before I did. After all, your field is investments, so you might have suggested I buy something else . . . ."

"Could be," she says, not wanting him to think she has a right to advise him on anything. But she realizes her opinion on his investments can't matter that much because he runs down her steps so quickly she can't ask for details. Where did he buy his RRSP? She'd have loved to sit next to him to discuss investments, his soapy smell enveloping her as their knees touched. Any excuse to get close. Just the thought makes her almost dizzy. Did he buy mutual funds or stocks? She pushes these thoughts from her mind, preferring to wonder what kind of movies he likes.

She misses seeing people succeed by taking her advice. She thinks of the Lovells, a couple who thought they'd have to work into their seventies until Adrienne invested them in blue-chip mutual funds. They bought a B&B and were able to hire a manager to run it when they travelled. Thoughts of successes like that make her angry someone else is now helping her clients.

The next day, sun bright and sky blue, Adrienne walks to the hairdresser's on St. Clair West, where she gets a trim and tint with gold highlights. At home, over a sandwich and wine, she looks up recipes in her seldom-used cookbooks. By the time she's finished another glass, her list includes artichoke dip, broccoli roll ups, and mushroom turnovers. As she's cautious about driving after drinking, she walks to get the ingredients and takes a taxi home. She decides, after putting away the food, to read more of her father's letters.

She stands in the dining room and notices the note that had first fallen out of Aunt Margaret's envelope. She realizes from reading so many of his letters that its much later date —1959 — makes it different from the others. She rereads this note out loud, as if hearing her own voice would clarify the meaning of the last two sentences: "I can't stop thinking about the dead. It's as if they're calling me to join them." Since discussing their meaning with Cass, she's spent a lot of time thinking about those lines. She knows, from television news or newspaper articles, what she now thinks they foretold. After the war, although it seems to have taken time to develop, he may have suffered from PTSD. She knows that more is understood about how soldiers involved in wars carry emotional scars for the rest of their lives. Today, she agrees with part of what Cass said. Because, in the letter, he says he thinks the dead are calling him to join them, he must have been obsessed with the cold bodies, blood congealed on their clothing, or limbs missing that he, as a doctor at the front, couldn't bring back to life.

She remembers how her father kept his patients' notes in school scribblers, probably because they were inexpensive. Maybe he wrote this note on paper torn from one of his scribblers when, as a psychiatrist, he was working with a war veteran to help him cope with his memories. It's so powerful in its reference to the dead, yet so unrelated to his other letters that she starts a pile of incongruous items, including some military insignia, pins, and ribbons. She'll keep them together, and when she's finished reading the letters, before she shows any of them to her mother, she'll mail these items back to Margaret and ask her about their meaning. Finally, she makes notes in her daybook: *buy plastic document holders, borrow genealogy book from local library*. If only she could find that diary Aunt Margaret wrote about in a letter. Where could it be?

She considers the possibility that her paternal grandmother snubbed Gloria. One memory she has of visiting her grandparents in London was after her mother and father had moved to Toronto. Her grandmother, Hanna Muir, was an elegant, grey-haired woman who ignored children. She expected her granddaughters to sit quietly in her living room before dinner and to disappear with a book after. She remembers her grandmother Muir one night when Cass fell asleep on the couch in her grandparents' library while Adrienne read her some A. A. Milne poems. Adrienne had returned to the living room where her parents were talking. When she asked her mother what the conversation was about, Hanna Muir interrupted in a voice that would silence the most talkative listener.

"Children should be seen and not heard."

Her grandmother was wearing a steel-blue dress, unlike the printed housedresses other grandmothers wore. Her eyes bore into Adrienne, but she said to her daughter-in-law, "Gloria, the girls need some manners." Adrienne knew better than to say she tried to be polite. Instead, her mother got up, took Adrienne's hand, and led her back to the library, where they stayed with Cass, who was sleeping, until her father claimed them.

She emerges from her thoughts about Hanna Muir when the phone rings. It's Barb Dawson, saying she'd heard about Adrienne leaving her job. Despite that, Barb needs her to arrange her son Josh's finances for when he starts university in the fall.

"I'm not working anywhere now," Adrienne says, "and before I take another job, I'm going to finish some research. But I'll find you someone."

"Thank you," Barb says. "That would be a big help."

After she hangs up, Adrienne brushes her teeth and goes to bed. As soon as her feet warm up, she falls asleep.

In the morning, Adrienne calls her old firm to say she won't tolerate them taking her clients. Whoever answers the phone doesn't recognize her name, and Adrienne is so incensed she hangs up and immediately redials Barb's number.

When she answers, Adrienne says, "I'm starting to sell financial products from home. If you don't mind, we can meet in my den."

"I don't want a new financial planner, so that's perfect. I have a while before Josh starts school, so let me know when you're ready and I'll come over."

Buoyed by Barb's enthusiasm, Adrienne begins to mentally list potential clients and what she needs to do to start a business. Then, if she gets another job, she can stop taking new customers and look after the ones she has, after hours.

In the kitchen, she pours a bit of scotch from the one bottle of Glenfiddich she's allowed herself since her drinking binge after losing her job and lines up the recipes for tomorrow's meeting. She's finished mixing the hot artichoke dip when the phone rings.

"Hi Adrienne," Cass says. "How are you adjusting to your extra time?"

"Right now, I'm cooking for my astronomy club. It's more of a break than an adjustment."

"If that's the case, I don't want to depress you, but after we discussed those letters you brought up here, I started to remember Dad. Could you confirm whether something happened that keeps repeating in my head?"

"Nothing's going to burn, so go ahead," says Adrienne, and takes a sip.

"Today, snow in the parking lot made me think of the time my class built an igloo for Winter Carnival. I think I was in Grade One. My class won a prize, but after they were given out . . . I remember . . . Dad took a golf club and knocked down the sculptures."

Adrienne sucks in a breath, which she thinks Cass has heard.

Her sister pauses then says, "When he finished, he was laughing . . . Did that happen?"

"I don't remember, but you could ask Mom."

"She'd just deny it."

"You're right," Adrienne says. "Denial is her first response . . . but I'll bet he did. He always was unpredictable. Sometimes even cruel."

"Did I fall asleep on his lap when he sat in his den?"

"I'm not sure, but Mom didn't like us to bother him when he worked at home."

"I know. She scolded me when she found me in his den and said I shouldn't bother him when he was working. But he'd just sit there . . . staring."

"He was concentrating," Adrienne says, but although she won't say it, she also thinks he was depressed. "Psychiatrists have a lot on their minds . . . and in them. I'm sorry, but I have to finish this food for my meeting." Then, not wanting Cass to feel dismissed, she adds, "If you remember anything more, call me."

"Sure," Cass says and hangs up.

Adrienne goes back to cooking and sipping. While flipping the mushroom turnover pastry, she thinks of her father destroying snow sculptures and believes what Cass remembers did happen. Suddenly, the sound of the doorbell interrupts her thoughts. At first, she considers not answering, but when she approaches the door, she sees through the side window that it's Tony.

After wiping her hands on her apron, she opens the door and says, "This is a pleasant surprise. I thought you'd wait until tonight then call me."

"I couldn't," he says, grinning.

"Don't you ever work?"

"I run, then do a few hours. What about you? When are you going to look for another job? You know, go back to work?"

"Right now, I'm cooking."

"Does this mean you'll be too busy for a movie, Saturday?" he teases.

"I'll be finished by then, so I could squeeze in *Pulp Fiction*."

"It sounds violent, but the reviews are good. I thought you'd choose a romantic comedy so we could laugh."

He shakes his arms and legs to keep warm, and Adrienne thinks his way of moving looks sexy.

"Laughing is good, but I have to cook. You should finish your run."

He starts down the steps, the streetlight haloing his greying curls.

"See you Saturday," she says.

He calls back, "Pick you up at six."

Back in the kitchen, she hopes she didn't sound harried. She wants this relationship to work, but she'd forgotten how much time such things take.

The next day, she sleeps late and scolds herself for getting into the scotch. By the time she drinks several coffees, showers, and packs the food, she's rushed, and, knowing she's late, finally sets out for her astronomy club meeting. Outside, snow blows across roadways and covers the ice beneath. Every time she brakes, the car slides sideways and the food containers in the back seat clink together, making her nervous about driving.

Dell lives in an old west-end area and has planned to take binoculars on a walk in High Park. Those who braved the snow nix the idea and congregate at the back of the house. Lucy, who's not five feet tall and a biology teacher on Toronto Island, and Norman, a chemist who's wearing a sulphurous-smelling lab coat, busy themselves with a telescope that sits near patio doors. Soon they're frustrated by heavy cloud cover and swirling snow. Dell, a computer analyst, and Joe, a real-estate agent, set folding chairs around the room so they can share log entries. Adrienne senses this meeting won't last long and asks Leon, a dentist who's visited observatories worldwide, to help with the food.

"In all the years I've come to these meetings, you've never brought anything," he says, following her to the kitchen.

"Dell was busy, so I said I'd help. I never had time to cook when I was working."

"Did you quit?"

"I got fired."

To avoid his reaction, she sticks her head in the fridge. He still looks shocked when she emerges, holding dip. She wishes she could shield people from their fears when they hear of another layoff.

"I was burned out anyway," she says reassuringly and puts the dip in the oven.

"Lucky you don't have kids. You'd be panicked." He sits down at the kitchen table.

"I don't consider that luck," she responds, and he lowers his eyes, blushing from collar to eyebrows. Quickly she adds, "Eventually, I'll need to find work, but for now, I'm okay, what with severance..."

"I couldn't go a month without pay. So, you must have done well in the market."

"I've been careful," she says and puts turnovers on a cookie sheet.

"Talking about this reminds me, it's February and tax time,

which always makes me anxious. Every year, I tell myself I'll invest for retirement, but I never do . . . I never have enough."

Leon helps her put out the snacks. The club members drink beer and eat as they read from their logs. Norman's been sick since their last meeting and has nothing to report. Dell was in Fiji and mentions nebulae he saw that Adrienne's never seen. The others seem genuinely interested in the stars she saw up north. If the sky weren't flooded with light, she'd see the same ones here, but she's glad she recorded the ones she saw on the road from Sudbury. At least she had something to say.

Without warning, Leon asks her how a financial wizard got interested in astronomy. Although she's rarely talked about her father outside the family, she finds herself describing how he'd introduced her to the Milky Way. Dell sets the next meeting's date: the last Friday of March at Lucy's Toronto Island house. A place that's excellent for observations. The talk turns to people's children, and Adrienne, though childless, is glad to mention her visit with Cass and Samantha. Everyone is worried about her lost job, vowing to ask friends about possible positions.

As she starts for the door, Lucy stops her and says, "Let's get together for lunch before the next meeting and dish about families. Mine was difficult, to say the least, and my relationship with my father was non-existent. But your father sounds different. I'd love to hear more about how you and he shared an interest in the stars."

Adrienne, who only knows Lucy from meetings, suddenly sees her as a friend and says, "Sure. He taught me everything I know. But we better set a date, or we won't do lunch."

They sit on the bench by the door and compare calendars.

"It'll have to be a Saturday. I teach all week," says Lucy, "and there isn't time to take the ferry across and back during the lunch hour."

"Let's do next Saturday. There's a nice fish restaurant down by the ferry dock, so it won't be hard for you to get back," says Adrienne. Yet, she knows she'll be reluctant to describe how, as her father's alcoholism got worse and worse, he lost all interest in the constellations and his wife and children.

After their dinner-and-a-movie date, which she hopes becomes a habit, Tony stands in his spot on her veranda.

"Thanks for a fun evening," she says, yawning. "Even though that film was pretty violent."

"That's an understatement," he says. "But the director is known for that. You seem tired."

"I am, but I need to summon some energy to take my niece to Florida for spring break. To visit my mother." She thinks that with John off sailing, Gloria might be more open to talking about her father's death, a topic about which she wants clarity.

"You just got back from North Bay . . . and I'll miss you," Tony says, leaning forward.

Their lips touch, and his face has a *how do I proceed?* look. She considers asking him in but remembers the hurt she felt when Graham left and doesn't want to rush more involvement, especially physical, so she decides to keep it light. Like their conversations have been so far. But he's already off down the steps.

"See you again soon," she calls after him.

September 14, 1943

Back from leave and now in Catanzaro hospital — no beds, water, power — no rain either — despite discomfort, glad to be dry and warm.

Got first mail since England — strange letter from Gloria wishing we hadn't married — if she were single, could teach — ridiculous — send enough money to decorate her apartment — soon be home, we'll try for another baby.

Mother and Father haven't seen Gloria — her parents told Mom that Gloria stayed in room for weeks after losing baby — I worry about how she has nothing to care for — sure she's terribly lonely and I'm not there to comfort her — might be help in her grief to talk to Val Thompson, her neighbour, husband killed in Sicily.

MacPhee got letter from sweetheart, Madge — shapely redhead, more willing than Gloria — Madge wrote she married Claude Dionne who lost leg in battle and came home.

MacPhee tore up letter — said Dionne dimwitted, would never know enough to satisfy Madge — thought she would wait so won't trust women again.

Children here starving so gave them our canned vegetable mush, biscuits, canned cheese — looks and tastes like soap — glad it's of use to hungry.

Typhus nearby — nurses, doctors scrubbing equipment — no medicine — most frightening medical thing so far, except death, in war — only thing for typhoid is prayer.

SIX

Gloria

John leans over Gloria's chair in the living room and kisses her hair, then switches on a lamp.

"What about dinner?" he asks and sits in his recliner. "Adrienne and Sam will be here soon, and they'll be hungry.

"I was too tired to think about it after hosting Bridge Club. I'll stick the casserole in now."

"Let's go out. I don't want to be here if Raymond calls."

Their old Toronto friends, Doris and Raymond, who also live in this Florida seniors' community during the winter, had an argument yesterday. It was overheard all the way from their first-floor apartment to the pool, where John, Gloria, and many of the other residents were sunning. If Doris knew that everyone in the community had heard, she'd be mortified.

"At bridge club, Doris wouldn't tell us anything about the fight."

"She's afraid people will talk," he says and gives his signature head bob.

"They already are, and it's probably about the wrong thing," Gloria says, trying to probe. She hopes John knows the story and will tell her, so she gets up and goes to the kitchen where she wipes the counters. Then she loads the dishwasher, and John folds the bridge chairs.

"Raymond told me that last night, Doris got the nerve to tell him she's been unhappy with their sex life since he returned from the war," he suddenly says when he's joined her in the kitchen.

"That's fifty years ago," Gloria says, pursing her lips. "No pun intended, but I'll bet the subject rarely comes up, and I'm surprised he told you that."

He winks and says, "Do people think that about us?"

"I doubt it. You're so affectionate . . ."

Certainly, their sex life has waned with age, and half of her is bolstering his ego, but the other half is telling the truth. Compared to Alex, who slept in their room while she slept elsewhere for much of their marriage, John could be described, even now, as amorous.

"Raymond says he makes love to Doris Saturday mornings," John says. His face is lowered so she can't see his eyes. "He used to reserve Wednesday evenings after bowling, but as they've gotten older, he says one morning a week is enough."

She thinks Raymond and John talk more about sex than she ever has with Doris, which is not surprising because she finds graphic talk vulgar.

"Although I dislike this kind of talk, I'll just add I'm surprised Doris is unhappy."

"It's not quantity, it's quality," John says as he rests his weight against the card table's edge. "And Raymond said Doris claims he's been like a robot since the war."

Gloria thinks John has finished talking when he adds, "When I got back, no one liked me. The Italian-Canadian girls thought I was a fascist. Yet when we met, you didn't judge me. You understood what war can do to men."

She's about to say, "I tried," when the front-hall intercom buzzes.

"That'll be Adrienne and Sam," John says. "Did you hide the liquor?"

"I won't play games. If she wants it, she'll find it."

As John goes to answer the door, Gloria sees he's walking gingerly. She hears the familiar "*merda*," under his breath and thinks his knees must hurt, so she doesn't scold. While Adrienne stands in the hall, Sam bursts into the condo, pulling her suitcase behind her. John motions Adrienne inside while Gloria looks on, smiling to herself that Adrienne looks happy to be visiting. Sam returns to the hall for another purse-like bag and, hearing her grandmother promise they'll eat out, says, "Burgers and fries, I hope."

"We prefer a buffet. That way everyone can choose."

"If Sam wants hamburgers," John says, his eyes wide, "to the closest fast-food place we'll go. Are we ready?"

"I think Mom and I'll stay here. You take Sam for burgers," Adrienne says. "I want to put up my feet."

To Gloria, the idea of staying home seems impolite, but she knows John wants to please Sam. When they leave, she hears them laughing all the way to the elevator.

She turns on the oven and puts an already prepared, stuffed-pepper casserole in it. Adrienne slices cucumbers for salad, while Gloria goes to change from her leisure suit to dress pants and a jacket. When she returns, her daughter has set the table, and the scent of seasoned tomatoes warms the kitchen.

"Where does John keep the wine?" Adrienne asks, struggling to tuck her shortened hair behind her ears.

"There's a half-bottle of Riesling in the fridge," Gloria says, hoping Adrienne will be satisfied with one glass. "When are you going to look for another job?"

"I'm taking time off to research Daddy's life, starting with his letters."

Gloria hears herself muttering as she moves several plates to fit the salad bowl into the dishwasher.

"Daddy mentioned you in one. After we clean up, I'll get it."

"Where did Margaret find them?"

"In the Muir's house. After Grandma Muir died, she found them in a trunk along with some pictures."

While Gloria wipes the stove with foaming cleanser, Adrienne sweeps the floor, then walks down the hall to her room for the letters. Gloria leans against the dining table, knees weak. She's tried, for years, not to think about Alex, and she doesn't want to think about him now. She doesn't ever want to think about the Muirs again. To her, their aloofness was a sign they thought themselves superior. Even now, that thinking makes her angry.

As a child, Gloria had heard shocking stories about her own extended family, the MacLeans, from under her parents' bedroom door. Such tales as how after Aunt Betsy, a minister's wife, ran off with a door-to-door salesman, and her husband found sherry bottles hidden in a drawer under her corsets, or how Cousin Dexter, a bachelor and Sunday School Superintendent, was said to prefer young boys. It took Gloria years to understand how he preferred them. Then there was Aunt Willa, a spinster, who was caught behind the barn naked to the waist with a farm hand, and Cousin Delores, a university English professor, who had a housekeeper named Sadie. Not until adulthood did Gloria understand what her mother meant by, "The only thing Sadie kept in Delores's house was Delores's bed warm." Drunks, pedophiles, nymphomaniacs, and lesbians, although never said aloud, were terms Gloria learned, some recently, to describe her relatives to herself. On the other hand, Hanna carted out her own Muir myths, coldly and predictably. To her, Cartwright Muir was a never celebrated doctor who'd helped diabetics by testing insulin on them in its early development. Imogene Muir was an artist who'd painted Muskoka along with the original Group of Seven. William Muir, an architect, designed what were to be Ottawa's first parliament buildings — until the drawings caught fire. Everyone she mentioned was wealthy and successful.

Early in their courtship, Gloria thought her family's ancestors were different from Alex's, who seemed a cut above. But when he died, his mother handed her a box saying, "Wear this. I won't have you shame me at my son's funeral." Hearing that, Gloria knew the Muirs weren't superior human beings; all Hanna cared about were appearances. As far as Gloria was concerned, despite having less money, her parents had more class than the Muirs.

Gloria is still mulling these memories when Adrienne returns with some papers.

"Reading them makes me sad, but I want to know more about him," she says and puts several pages on the table then sits down.

"Would you like some coffee?"

"No thanks. I had some on the plane. You look anxious," Adrienne says, pulling out the chair next to her for her mother. "Why don't you want to read them?"

"I hate remembering his death. It wasn't pleasant."

"I'm sure it wasn't. After all, you loved him. But these letters are from before he died."

Gloria doesn't answer. She's never told her daughters their father was an alcoholic, hoping this secret would preserve his image. Despite feeling that if she reads the documents she might end up saying too much, she sits down and opens the first one. Monogrammed stationary falls out.

"There's a letter from me to the Muirs included in this envelope as well, but read the one from Daddy when he was studying in Toronto."

Toronto General Hospital
July 13, 1941

Dear Mother and Father,

Hot, humid air covers Toronto like a damp blanket. I need a drive in the country to cool off, like we used to when London got hot.

After doing my first tonsillectomy, another intern and I celebrated with dinner at Fran's and a frat party. I barely got up this morning.

I hope Gloria's parents let her visit me this summer. I think they're angry that I proposed to her without asking them. I thought that if we were engaged, Mr. MacLean would know that my intentions toward her were honourable. Then he would let his daughter visit me.

Love, Alex

Gloria looks up from reading when Adrienne again asks, "Why are you afraid?"

"I don't want you to think less of your father."

"I hardly knew him, so that's not going to happen. Why didn't your parents want you to visit him?"

"They were old-fashioned and thought we should marry before we spent time . . . unchaperoned," Gloria says and presses her index fingers against her temples, as if soothing a headache.

"How soon after this letter was the wedding?"

"The following summer." Gloria's cheeks are damp. "Of course, I wished we could have gone somewhere wonderful for our honeymoon, but the war was on, so your father and I reported to army camp."

"That makes sense."

"Despite the shabby married quarters' barracks, your father tried to be . . . romantic. He spent time with me when he could, but the soldiers spent more time on drinking and war games than they did on their brides."

"Liquid courage, they say. They were afraid to go to war. Now, read the next letter."

107 Roxborough Drive,
Toronto, Ontario
January 8, 1960

Dear Grandma and Grandpa Muir,

Thank you for the presents. Grandma MacLean made me wait until my birthday to open them. The pink angora sweater set is beautiful. I also like the china cups you gave me for my hope chest. I'll have to get one. I still take piano lessons after school. I hope to have my birthday party in a few weeks. I had to cancel it this week because Mommy is away. Thank you again.
Love your granddaughter,
Adrienne

Her daughter had written this letter three days after her father died. His parents insisted on him being buried in the family's London plot, so she gave in to their wishes, which meant that, later, she had to go to London to visit his grave.

"That was two days after my birthday, after Daddy died," says Adrienne. "Grandma MacLean was looking after us. She told me what to write. I had to cancel my party until you got back. Why didn't we go?"

"Children didn't go to funerals, then," her mother says.

She knows her answer is absurd and considers telling more,

like what a good job the funeral director did on Alex's body, how his head looked normal, and that his mother had him laid out in a beautifully tailored suit. But because she's kept so much of this secret, she knows she'll never feel comfortable telling.

"And why didn't I mention his death in the letter?"

"People thought it best not to talk about such things. If they weren't mentioned, they'd be forgotten." Gloria places her daughter's note on the table and stands up.

"If we'd gone to the funeral, I might have grieved. Seeing people cry might have helped me be more open . . . more mature . . . about things like my divorce."

"I hate talking about your father." Gloria wants Adrienne to change the subject and talk about what "more mature" means to her, but instead she says, "I've never accepted his death, so how can you? He died . . . I won't have John catch us talking about this. He's got enough things to think about."

"And just what are those?" Adrienne asks. Although there are more letters in the pile next to her, she folds them together as if she won't bother showing Gloria more.

"Our friends, Raymond and Doris, are arguing. Raymond won't go sailing until it's settled, so John doesn't have a sailing buddy." Once again, she presses her forehead with her fingertips to quell her headache, then starts down the hall. "Now, I'm going to bed. I'm sure I'll feel better in the morning."

John wakes Gloria with a gentle shake.

"Thinking about Doris and Raymond's problems wore me out," she says.

"You won't enjoy Adrienne's visit if your nerves are frayed," he says and gets her a sleeping pill, which she washes down with the tea he brought.

"What will Adrienne and Sam do while I sleep?"

"I'll show them the boat. If Raymond and I go sailing, the girls can come. Or they can shop. I'll bring home dinner. But I have to call Raymond, tell him something."

From the bedside phone, she hears him say that Raymond should agree to sex therapy, to help the marriage.

"Just get it over with so we can go sailing."

Gloria has never thought of Raymond as a candidate for therapy, sexual or otherwise. Instead, she's wondered, more than once, how Doris can stand listening to his nostalgic stories yet again and find the energy to feign interest. Drifting off, she considers how her friend kept a secret from Raymond for years. During all that time, sexual gratification didn't matter, but then something changed her mind and made her tell.

She thinks of her own secrets. How she, not wanting to criticize his gift giving abilities, replaces John's presents of *White Shoulders* perfume by pouring out the liquid, rinsing the bottle and refilling it with *Chanel No. 5*. Or the secrets about their father she's kept from her children, like the lost key. Things no good could come from telling. In the whole scheme of life, did it seem fair to hurt good people by revealing unnecessary things?

She lets sleep capture her and spends the day drifting in drug-induced dreams. Alex is there, his car idling at the curb. Her parents, Moira and Duncan MacLean, greet him. They think Alex is spoiled with money and gets everything he wants. They also expect Gloria to be chaperoned while she's at his grandparents' farm, and they tell him so. During haying, Alex drives a tractor while she helps in the kitchen. Britain declares war the last summer Alex is at home, but Gloria believes it will end soon. Then, she's in her parents' kitchen. With war looming and Alex alive, he's her best hope for a family. When she asks her parents if she can visit him in Toronto now that they're engaged, she'll never forget her father's response.

"You won't spend two weeks alone with that man. And you won't have my blessing."

He never sees, even after their satin and lace, lily-of-the-valley wedding at Hillview, that marrying Alex gave her something to remember in case he died at war and she had to go on living without him.

When the phone next to her bed rings, her tongue feels as thick as beefsteak.

Doris begins with, "I told Raymond not to talk to me unless it's with a therapist. He hasn't said a word."

"Oh," Gloria says. "You woke me."

"Sorry," Doris says, "I can call back."

"No . . . Give him time. You know men and their egos. It must be hard for them to admit their sexual prowess isn't . . . perfect."

"To be precise, it's not the quantity but the quality that's the problem."

"What I've wondered is why you told him in the first place."

"After that Sex and Seniors lecture we heard, I decided I wanted to enjoy sex. You know . . . have an orgasm before I died. I didn't know what else to do."

Gloria's mouth drops open. She'd sat next to Doris at that talk, but she never dreamt *this* was the problem. Considering how upset Raymond's been, Gloria thought it was probably an old man's problem: prostate, impotence, or incontinence, those inevitable signs of aging. Instead, it was Doris. In women's magazines, Gloria's read about self-administered pleasure, with devices, but to her the idea is as unspeakable as having an affair outside of marriage.

"Go to therapy," she finally says, "so we won't have to talk about this anymore and the men can go sailing."

"Fine," Doris sniffs. "I'll talk to Martha from bridge. She nursed soldiers during the war and married an Italian grape grower who worked nude in his vineyard . . . where they often had sex. She'll know what to do."

"Good. And call me if you want tea." What a rarity! Gloria's found a topic she doesn't like discussing with Doris. Sex talk should only be between partners. The safest place for her is in bed. She turns down the phone, rolls over and goes back to sleep.

The light flicks on, and Gloria sees her granddaughter and Adrienne at the foot of the bed holding shopping bags.

"It's dinnertime," Sam says, "and I want to show you my stuff."

Gloria, who hasn't brushed her teeth in twenty-four hours,

feels so grubby she knows eating in the dining room is impossible until she's had a bath.

"Show me your things, and Adrienne can bring me supper."

Sam pulls the clothes she's bought out of shopping bags from high-end stores. A black bra and thong underwear for a fourteen-year-old surprise Gloria.

"I meant to call your mother and tell her you got here safely. I'll call her now and ask her what she thinks of thong-style underpants for you."

"It's okay. Aunt Adrienne bought them for me."

"Hmm . . . All right then. You go and help John set the table."

Soon, Adrienne comes back carrying a tray. She lifts a blue-and-white checked cloth napkin, revealing chicken parmesan, pasta, and a salad. An envelope is tucked under her plate. The card inside reads, *We've been friends since you met John. Let's ignore what's between Raymond and me and go shopping soon. Love, Doris*. Gloria smiles and replaces it in the envelope without saying a word.

Adrienne points to the pill bottle on the bedside table and says, "If you're sick, we should call a doctor."

"I'm not. I just needed to sleep. I don't need any more pills, but you buying Sam that revealing underwear surprised me."

"Oh mother. Things have changed. Girls grow up sooner. I wouldn't have bought them if I thought Cass would disapprove. Eat your dinner, and tomorrow, when you're rested, we can look at another letter."

For two more days, Gloria feigns exhaustion to avoid the letters, while Adrienne and Sam tour St. Petersburg. John waits while Doris and Raymond settle things. Then they go sailing. On the third night, she consents to eat on the balcony.

Over coffee and dessert, Adrienne says, "John and I want to look at the stars from the boat tonight, so we rented you a movie."

"And we've got pop and chips for the show," Sam adds. "Or we could play Scrabble."

John turns off the barbecue and says, "Okay ladies. Let's load up the dishwasher and get started."

While the movie, *Fried Green Tomatoes*, plays, Gloria contemplates not having lived close to Sam while she was growing up. Shopping for her granddaughter's clothes and doing her hair would have been fun. They could have gone to museums and talked about what they saw. That's how a grandmother gets to know a grandchild. Gloria wishes she hadn't been so angry at Cass about moving north. Considering she's been to almost every country in Europe, if she'd been willing to travel to North Bay, she could have been more a part of Sam's childhood. John would have liked that, too.

When the film is over, Sam takes the well-worn Scrabble box out of the cabinet. She sets the board on the coffee table, and they draw tiles. Gloria gets the first word.

"My mom says you won't talk about her father. Why's that, Grandma?"

"Talking about him doesn't feel good."

"I learned in school to say no to things that don't feel good . . . but, it makes my mother feel bad that you won't talk about her father. That's why, when I ask about my father, she talks about him," Sam says. Then, she sets down the word ZINNIA, which puts her ahead.

"I'll tell you what I know about your father. The few times I met him, I liked him."

"You can call him Eric. That's how he signs his letters to my mom and me."

"I didn't know he wrote you," Gloria says and wonders whether his letters will someday haunt Cass as Adrienne's reading of Alex's letters worry her — in case her daughter discovers something she'd kept secret.

Sam picks up points by covering triple letter scores. After several more turns, she's winning.

"He writes to me for my birthday, Christmas, and sometimes in between." Sam pauses to eat a chip. "And he sends emails, which are a new thing that I had to learn how to write. Right now, he's working at the International Red Cross's headquarters, but his last email sounded like he wanted to come home. Why do people have to go so far away to do something they think is important?"

"Your father wanted your mother to join him in helping people who were less fortunate, but your mother wanted to be a professor and look after you."

"If he cares about the world, why doesn't he care about me?"

"He does, or he wouldn't write. And your mother says he's been putting money away for your education, so he's thinking about your future." Gloria is thankful for this, as she's certain Cass hasn't saved any. Although she doubts lack of thrift is an inherited trait, she wonders whether Cass adopted this attitude from her father.

"Mom says the same thing about him."

Gloria feels her chin bobbing on her chest. She opens her eyes, and Sam is announcing that she's won.

"Leave it set up so John and Adrienne can look at your words," Gloria says and goes to brush her teeth.

John stands at the end of their bed the next morning and says, "Sam and I are going to baseball, spring training. You need to get up and move around."

"Aren't you and Raymond going sailing?" Gloria wants the men to leave so she can persuade Doris to come for tea. That way, Adrienne will have to stop her incessant questions.

"He and Doris are doing sensitivity training, whatever that is. And I sailed enough last night."

"What a night it was," Adrienne says, joining them. "We saw Cancer, the open cluster called the Manger, Puppis at Argo's stern, and Corvus, the raven."

Adrienne's awed tone reminds Gloria of Alex's voice, long ago, when he talked about stars, before he lost interest in everything. The night he proposed, while they waited for his train, he pointed out the constellation named after Delphinus. Poseidon had put her among the stars for taking charge of his wedding. At the time, Gloria thought she'd never forget the details of that myth, but she has. She blames it on Alex's dying. If he couldn't keep living, she couldn't keep remembering.

With her voice breaking, she asks, "John, did you like the stars as much as Adrienne did?"

"After I remembered how to use them to navigate, which I learned in the war, we had fun. Now, how about you get up so you and Adrienne can visit and Sam and I can watch baseball."

From his intent face, Gloria knows she can't make excuses today.

"Let me get into the tub," she says and waves them away.

"I'll fill it up for you while John gets breakfast," Adrienne says and goes to the adjoining bath.

While standing in the kitchen with Adrienne later, Gloria says, "Before I took that sleeping pill, John told me you and he may go into business."

"I told him I don't like charging friends when they ask for financial advice, but I felt weird giving it for free," Adrienne says. "He said he'd help me figure out when to charge and bring me clients. Going into business is his idea, not mine, but because he's my stepfather, I'll think about it."

"You couldn't find a better partner than John."

"I'm sure you're right," she says and slides yellowed papers from under the toaster oven. She hands them to Gloria and asks, "How does this letter make sense?"

"You know I hate reading these, but I guess you won't stop, so I have to."

Toronto General Hospital
October 4, 1941

Dear Mother and Father,

Thank you for the cheque. After my appendectomy, it helped me pay my debts. About my allowance: now that I'm engaged, I need more money.

I wasn't able to start back until a few days ago. Since then,

I've been working from 7 p.m. to 7 a.m., so I sleep during the day. Please don't tell Gloria about my operation. She'll just worry. It'll be soon enough to tell her when we're married and she sees the scar. Margaret came every night while I was ill, and a few interns stopped by every time she was there. None caught her eye the way you'd hoped. Perhaps she'll end up single, but it won't be because of her looks or her personality.

You and Grandpa can get this money business settled at the farm on Sunday. Grandpa and Grandma Muir like having Gloria with them, and they think we'll be happy.
Love, Alex

They stare at each other across the kitchen.

"What's this about his parents not telling you he'd had appendicitis?" Adrienne finally asks.

"In those days, men thought sickness was for sissies. Besides, the Muirs rarely told me anything." On saying this, Gloria remembers how, when her parents-in-law picked her up at the train for Alex's funeral, she asked Hanna where the service would be held.

"It's not your concern," she'd said, her mouth pinched. "I've arranged everything."

Gloria kept silent about the service, though she didn't believe Alex would have wanted a church-affiliated funeral. He'd told her he'd felt abandoned by God while at war, so he would have dismissed a church funeral service as a sham.

"What about the diary you gave Daddy?"

"I gave him handkerchiefs and socks. Maybe a diary. If he wrote in it, he didn't show me," Gloria says, then leaves the kitchen.

Adrienne follows her to the living room. She reaches into her pocket and pulls out her father's scrap paper letter. Pointing to the lines "I can't stop thinking about the dead. It's as if they're calling me to join them," she asks, "What does this mean?"

"How do I know? It's probably a reference that shows how depressed he was. He was consumed with dark thoughts about things that happened to him during the war, and he felt guilty that he couldn't save more lives. It looks like it was torn from a workbook he used for his patients' notes. Besides, this letter was to his mother. They were close. I used to think he told her more than he told me, so it's too bad she's gone, or you could ask her."

Adrienne's eyes roll upward as she says, "If asking you about my father is pointless, I'll take Sam to Disneyworld rather than waste time talking to you." When her mother doesn't respond, she continues, anger straining her voice. "We'll go after John and Sam get back. Then we'll come back Thursday, to catch the plane."

"You don't understand. I've got to consider John."

Adrienne shoves hair behind her ears angrily and says, "Your life with John is solid. He wouldn't mind if you talked about my father to me."

"Perhaps, but right now I'm tired. I'm going to take a nap," and Gloria turns and walks away.

"That's always your response, Mother," Adrienne calls after her, but Gloria keeps walking. She knows that if her daughter's questions and unrelenting insistence on her reading her father's letters continue, she may have to re-examine her memories of the day of his death, which will be painful. As the weeks pass, her recollections become more clouded by her desire not to be judged by her daughters, something that seems more likely every passing day.

October 3, 1943

Wintry weather decreases dysentery but increases hepatitis, depression — things so grim, can hardly get up to continue.

Moved to Lucera school — 110 patients admitted, many casualties — many beds, no mattresses, pillows — nothing for casualties to die on — glad of morphine for patients and myself — didn't sign up for war without essentials to practice medicine.

Nazis rescued Mussolini, re-established fascist government — Jewish schoolteacher here was resistance leader, removed from classroom, forced onto train for camp — rumoured Jews taken North, disappear, perhaps buried in mass graves, otherwise what would Nazis do with numbers — another brutality of this already vicious war — wrote Gloria that her sadness normal — no letter in return — lost baby pains like knife in her heart — my heart hurts too — looked forward to holding my first child — will we ever be happy again?

SEVEN

CASS

On the Thursday before March Break, after putting Sam on a plane for Florida, Cass drives to work, hoping to finish her marking before her daughter returns. In the hallway, she meets Sharon, her best friend at the university and a tenured psychology professor. Although Cass teaches sociology, which Sharon might dismiss as a study of generalizations, she knows Sharon respects her writings. To return that feeling, as she knows Sharon's area of expertise is teen suicide, and she's recently published an academic article about that very subject, Cass asks where she can find it in the university library.

"*Psych/Soc Digest*" she says. "If you read it, let me know what you think. You might be the only person, other than one or two of my students, who looks at it."

"I will while Sam's in Florida."

"While she's away, come for dinner then a movie. I'll call you." And she hurries off, carrying a stack of papers.

All morning, Cass grades *Social Problems* papers. Her top student's essay quotes single-parent family statistics and says that a family of two, earning much less than her, lives above the poverty line. Yet, with a teenager to feed, clothe, entertain, and educate, along with herself, both having high-end tastes, she's without a house, has no savings outside her pension, and only takes trips to her mother's for vacations. On the other hand, Adrienne, who's jobless, can afford to take Sam to Florida. Maybe it's time to finally get serious about finances.

After teaching her *Industrial Sociology* class, Cass is back in her office reading Sharon's article, which she's borrowed from the library, instead of grading papers. The first paragraphs quote teen suicide statistics and give warning signs: listlessness, insomnia or excess sleep, loss of appetite, weight gain, and mood swings from buoyancy to depression. If Sam skies Saturday, she's listless Sunday. When she watches TV late, she sleeps in the next day. If the menu includes squash, she loses her appetite. For a moment, Cass remembers her own teenage years, how she loved O'Henry chocolate bars and gained twenty pounds during high school, how before her periods, she was depressed, and how if she stayed up past midnight studying, she could barely get up the next day. Finally, she reassures herself that Sam appears to be basically happy and is a fairly normal teenager.

Cass's head begins to bob against her chair back after reading the paper. She fights against sleep, knowing she has work to do, but her eyes close as she slumps into her chair. Suddenly, she hears a tremendous bang, then her mother's voice says, "Stupid fool. Cleaning your gun. You nearly shot her." With that, Cass opens her eyes, shakes her head to clear it then sits up. Some daydream, she thinks. More like a nightmare. Or was it a flashback? She puts her head down on her desk to rest. Then, she goes to the staff room and makes a cup of chamomile tea, which she takes back to her office and drinks, breathing deeply. Finally, she pushes away any remnants of that dream and tells herself she has to mark papers. By late afternoon, the *Social Problems* essays are graded for Friday's class, which makes her feel like she's in control of at least her job, if not her finances.

Outside, snow pelts the parking lot. She starts her car, and while it warms up, she whisks her windows. As she stands knee deep in snow, the tops of her boots fill with icy water and slide down to her ankles, making them hurt. One of her fellow professors, who has arthritis, told her damp, snowy weather makes his pain worse; she hopes that isn't happening to her.

On her way home, she sees two cars in the ditch. She slows down, inching over black ice, as the other automobiles in front of her move like snails. Relieved when she finally arrives in her kitchen, she heats a can of tomato soup, making it with milk for added nutrition. While sipping the warm liquid, she opens the paper and, halfway in, sees the horoscopes. Under her sign, Cancer, she reads, "Pay attention to family. Take stock of your finances. Invest in a home or renovate the one you own." With Sam away, she can't attend to family, but after this afternoon's thoughts, looking at her finances is probably a good idea. Adrienne said she should buy a house, and after reading March 1995 *North Bay Nugget*'s real-estate section, she'll need $6,700 down for the tiniest home on the list, which is more than she's ever had in savings. She knows owning a home is just a dream, and because she doesn't want to ask Adrienne or her mother for financial help, like her father had relied on his family, she turns to the headlines.

Vietnam commemorates 27th anniversary of My Lai massacre in Low Key Ceremony.

Twenty-seven years ago, she was in grade ten and fifteen years old. At first, she was horrified by the bloody Vietnam War she had to watch on TV every night for a school assignment. Later, she watched it because she was spellbound.

Her mother was dating John then, and Adrienne had night classes at U. of T., so Cass did homework with the television for company. She's never forgotten the naked girl, running down a road, her skin burned from Napalm. Just then, John and her mother returned from dinner and saw the girl on the screen. That night, Cass first heard John whisper his signature invective "*merda*," which, from studying French, she deduced meant "shit" in Italian.

Soup downed, she scans the obituaries for familiar surnames. As she doesn't recognize anyone, she reads her mail. The first envelope has a *remit immediately* sticker on its outside. Another bill threatens small claims court. A notice announces she's in overdraft.

She'll have to meet that patronizing woman at her bank to fix the deficit. At the bottom of the pile is a letter from her sister, mailed before Adrienne and Sam went to Florida.

She could have emailed me, thinks Cass. Adrienne's old firm quickly adopted this new form of communication, and she could send emails from her office. But, since leaving there, she'll have to hire a technician to install the technology on her home computer. Briefly, Cass is thankful that the IT department at her college helped her to get and send email at both her home and office.

She opens the envelope and chuckles to herself, knowing that Adrienne is using her manners to send a bread-and-butter note on a flower covered card. According to their mother, a thank you note after an overnight visit to someone's home is required. Folded inside the card is a sheet covered in Adrienne's handwriting and some other pages.

March 13, 1995

Dear Cass,

Thank you for your hospitality. You're right, I need email at home, as writing you that way would be simpler than writing a letter. However, I'm not sure, according to our mother's etiquette rules, it would pass as a correct thank you note. I really enjoyed getting to know you two again in North Bay. Taking Sam to Florida will be fun. It'll give you some time alone. You'll probably get this while we're away.

I found these pages in Aunt Margaret's package. You wrote the letter to our Muir grandparents after Daddy died. Grandma and Grandpa MacLean stayed with us in Toronto while Mom took his body to London for burial. I thought your letter was cute; you were a dear little girl, and I loved you very much.

I won't send Sam home until the Sunday after we return. You'll have a break, and she can give you her verdict on Tony. Since last week, I've eaten with him every day. If he becomes a habit, I might get hurt, so I'm glad to be away for a while with Sam on this trip. Travelling will give me something else to think about.
Love, Adrienne

Adrienne's hesitancy at getting involved with a man makes sense. To Cass, romance and getting hurt have always gone together. As soon as Eric Swanson persuaded her to trust him, her life became more difficult. She still remembers the future-changing conversation they'd had in that restaurant on Bloor, after a morning in the university library.

"Before we graduate with our MAs," he'd said, stirring two packages of sugar into his milk-laden coffee, "let's apply to do PhDs. If we get in, I think we should get married. I know for a fact that married students can get more money in student grants."

"Oh my," Cass had said. "Is this a proposal?" She'd felt herself blushing and was so surprised she couldn't speak, but she knew she had to answer. "I'm not . . . ." Then, she'd stopped.

"Life doesn't give guarantees," he'd said, his spectacles slipping down his nose. "I love you, and I think you love me. We'll help each other 'til we figure it out. Okay?"

During the slow silence that followed that moment, memories of her parents' marriage flooded her brain like blood from a burst aneurism. She recalled the day her father stopped eating dinner with his family and no longer shared chatter about the day's events, stopped reading his children bedtime stories, choosing instead to sit in his den and drink. She took a deep breath and told herself, this is not the kind of marriage I'm going to have. This is not going to happen to me.

Finally, fearing Adrienne would call her negative if she refused, she'd said, "Okay. But, because there's no one else to pass it on, I'm keeping my maiden name." Then, they'd shared such a passionate kiss that restaurant patrons stopped talking and stared. The silence caused Cass and Eric to break into uncontrollable laughter, and the diners closest to them clapped, giving the engagement an informal blessing.

There'd never been any question of how she loved spending time with Eric. His field was political science, which dovetailed well with hers: sociology. They both enjoyed reading and discussing each other's' writings, and they often lingered in bed, making love until long past noon. In the end, she deduced that marrying him was a natural progression. During the five years it took them to get their doctorates, Eric talked about going abroad to do international aid work. For as long as Cass had known him, he'd volunteered to help the less fortunate by sorting clothes at the Salvation Army, reading to pupils at the local primary school, and shovelling snow for seniors.

When they finally graduated, he said, "I've been offered a contract with the International Red Cross. They'll send me wherever I want to go that they work. I'm sure you can teach wherever we go."

As the thought of living somewhere exotic appealed to her, and the anthropologist Margaret Mead's writings on Samoa came to mind, she thought she could continue her research if she went with Eric. But, after she applied for teaching jobs in El Salvador, where he was assigned, the fighting there was so intense she decided, even if there were jobs, she wouldn't move. Then, when the offer came from Nipissing, where she'd also applied, she persuaded herself their love for each other was so strong he'd move back to Canada if they were separated for too long. She took the job in North Bay.

Now she remembers how Eric had said, "We'll help each other 'til we figure it out." As far as she is concerned, they both have a lot more to figure out. It wouldn't be as difficult for Sam if they began living with Eric as getting to know John was for Cass. She always thought, while she and Adrienne were teens, her mother wouldn't get involved with a man. According to Gloria, her daughters came first. So, when her mother was dating John, watching them kiss made her squirm. When they decided to marry, Cass realized she'd expected too much of her mother, and she came to love John, too, because he didn't intrude in her life.

Cass picks up the pink, scalloped pages from inside Adrienne's card and wonders where she got this elaborate stationary. The note contains all the elements of a properly written letter, including the return address of her childhood home, which indicates an adult probably helped her with it. If she remembers correctly, it was Grandma MacLean.

107 Roxborough Drive
Toronto, Ontario
January 8, 1960

Dear Grandma and Grandpa Muir,
Thank you for the skirt and sweater. I like the ice skates too. Mommy gave me this pretty note paper. I sang in a school concert. Adrienne can't have her party, and she's sad.
Love Cassandra XOX

Her paper question is answered. Then Cass remembers that Adrienne had some writing paper like this too, but it was light blue with darker blue lining the scalloped edges. It must have come from her mother, who always made sure that her gifts to her daughters were the same, or at least of equal value. She reads the letter again and notes the correct sentences and punctuation. Maybe she is a born professor. From the date, she calculates she wrote it when she was seven and in Grade Two. Then she wonders what party it mentions. Recalling that Adrienne was born in January, Cass thinks it must have been for her sister's birthday, which had to be cancelled because their father died. Surprisingly, the letter doesn't mention his death.

She could still hear her mother say, "Don't talk about him."

"Why not? He *was* my father."

"If we don't, the sadness will go away."

This letter, written by a girl who didn't understand, at the time, that her father's death meant she'd never see him again, makes her cry. Later, when she soaks every tissue from the box on her desk and needs to calm herself, she decides to check her email. Maybe some juicy gossip will stop her from thinking about herself. Besides some work-related messages, there's one from Eric.

TO: Cass
SUBJECT: New Job

Hi Cass:

Guess what? I've been offered a position with Global Insight in Vancouver, which, if I accept, would mean moving home. You know that moving to British Columbia is my dream. If this comes true, I'd like you both to come and live with me. You could get a job, but you must know I've been saving money with this in mind, so you'd only need to teach if you wanted to. Tell me what you think.
Love, Eric

Cass gets up and paces the hall, trying to absorb what she's read. Excited by these possibilities, she decides that if he accepts the job, she'll be willing to move and try marriage again. Her memories of their nightly lovemaking make her face flush. She knows sleeping together would reignite that fire. To the question of teaching — hasn't she done it for years? The job feeds her and Sam and could provide more if she didn't spend her salary before she got it. It also gives her something useful to do, and it will when Sam goes away to university, the cost made possible if they both work. Together, they could buy a house and soon pay off the mortgage. Although he might be tired of it, they could travel — something she's always wanted to do. She could decorate Sam's bedroom like a girl's room should be. Dreams fill her head, and she's thrilled that her daughter might finally get to know her father better —which she, herself, never could because her own father had died. Besides, she'd be living with the man she loved.

The next morning at the bank, Cass describes her monthly expenditures, and the manager puts figures into her computer. Finally, she says in a disdainful tone, "We can loan you some money, but you need to stop using your high-interest credit cards. I'll help you apply for our bank's lower interest card, but you need to pay cash when you can. And you need to pay the card's balance in full every month."

Cass's only response is "When will I get the money?"

"By Monday. I'll tell Toronto not to bounce any of your cheques." Then, handing her a budget she's printed from the computer, she pats Cass on the back and says, "Stick to this, and you'll be fine."

Cass strolls along Main Street to her car, thinking if Eric actually moves back to Canada and they reunite, she won't feel lonely for adult company anymore. Her women friends from the university are great, but being able to talk to someone besides Sam over the breakfast table, day after day, would be wonderful. She stares into store windows showing stuffed lambs and remembers Easter is coming. Inside the drug store, buying stamps with her credit card, she recalls the bank lady's advice and finds enough coins in her purse to pay outright. Tonight, she'll write cheques on the loaned money, then she'll use cash for Sam's chocolate. She'll resist her habit of charging new Easter clothes and shoes for them both and not paying the balance when the statement comes.

Cass recalls, before driving to the university Saturday morning, some loonies she'd squirreled away in a jar, hoping their value would increase with time as the silver dollar did. She slips them into her pocket, thinking if she could pay off her debts, she could easily save the amount these coins are worth every month. After all, she has to start somewhere.

On her way to the school, she orders a bagel and medium black at the drive-through window and uses the loonies to pay. With change in her pocket and payments on her dash, she has the same feeling of control she gets when she hands back marked papers. Buying things on impulse, like new furniture and clothes, has been her habit, but she hasn't had the urge for at least forty-eight hours.

While eating the bagel in her office and marking the last assignments, her mind keeps wandering. She looks out the window and sees that some winter-mad student has built a snowman on the parking lot's edge. She puts down her cup and turns her back on the lot. She'd believed, or maybe convinced herself, that she could block out memories of her father, as her mother had wanted her to do years ago. But when she sees the snowman, she remembers the winter carnival. With this recurring flashback, and the one she had of nearly being shot, she knows she'll never be able to forget him. But then again, maybe she shouldn't try. Instead, she should think of the good things she remembers about him.

Yet, she can't help asking herself, when he'd laughed as he knocked down the sculptures, was he feeling almost manic? She thinks of 'manic' as a psychological term. And later, when he'd sit alone in his den for days without speaking, was he depressed? Yet another psychological term. If she puts those two ideas together now, she can wonder whether her father might possibly have been manic-depressive. He could also, quite simply, have been chronically depressed. She knows drinking heavily can cause that effect and it's a more likely diagnosis. Either one of these verdicts is probably not out of the question. Whatever she names his behaviour, she knows he was erratic, which she's sure was fuelled by alcohol.

At home, she remembers she hasn't answered Eric's email. If she truly hopes to reconcile her marriage, she needs to reply.

TO: Eric Swanson
SUBJECT: Exciting

Hi Eric,

How wonderful that you might move to Vancouver. Both Sam and I would consider moving there. If I can't get a teaching job and we don't move, Sam and sometimes I would visit you in the summers. Let me know as soon as you make your plans.
Love, Cass

She's tried to make her reply open-ended, so Eric won't assume a move for her is inevitable. But after she presses the send button, she thinks that if Sam spends summers with Eric, she might love living there and want to go to a Vancouver school. Soon she'll be of legal age to make her own decision about where and with whom she wants to live. That thought makes her sit at the computer for several minutes and think about living without Sam. She knows she'd be unspeakably lonely.

Finally, she goes to the kitchen and fills the dishwasher, starting it immediately.

The water rushing through the pipes makes so much noise she barely hears the phone.

"Guess what, Mom," Sam says. "We're in Orlando and here's the number."

"Your Grandmother must be feeling better to go there," Cass says as she writes down the information.

"She didn't come. Last night, when Grandpa and I got home from baseball, Aunt Adrienne and I left. Grandpa seemed upset, but Aunt Adrienne said it was okay. Our hotel has a pool, and tomorrow we're going to Disneyworld."

"That sounds great. I love you. Now, could I talk to your aunt?"

"Hi," Adrienne says. "I've only got a minute. Sam's gone to the bathroom."

"What happened?"

"Mom was giving me the silent treatment about our father, and considering that wasn't the only reason I brought Sam here, I decided to get moving."

"About those memories," Cass says, but Adrienne interrupts with, "Here's Sam, ready to go."

"Let me say goodbye," Cass says, hearing Sam's voice in the background.

"I'll bring you a Mickey Mouse hat." Then she's gone.

Cass sits in Sharon's kitchen at an old high-school desk, painted and enlarged with a plywood top, making it a table. There is so little space that Sharon serves the chili from a pot on the stove.

"If you don't mind me asking, how does this house compare to the one for sale next door?"

"That place is bigger but cost less. It needs work: plumbing, electrical...you know," says Sharon, her eyebrows arched. "This one didn't need fixing, but all I could scrape together was a down payment. Because I hate being in debt, I had to forego furniture."

Cass becomes thoughtful for a minute, considering whether she should adopt that philosophy of no debt and how her whole life would have to change. By the time she finishes paying for the couch she just bought, she'll need a new one. But she knows that even if she had to buy a new table on time, she'd pay the incurring interest rather than dine at this makeshift one.

"Have you heard from Sam?" asks Sharon as she serves salad from the counter.

"Last night. Sam and Adrienne went to Disneyworld, minus Mom."

"Is there trouble in paradise? Not that Florida is, if you ask me."

Cass has never minded talking honestly to Sharon, so she explains how Adrienne is questioning their mother's story about their father's death, how their mother won't answer truthfully, and how Sam knows the question of how her grandfather died is still causing problems in the family.

"I thought your mother *and* father wintered in Florida."

"Stepfather . . . for twenty-five years. My biological father died when Adrienne and I were young."

"And Adrienne wants to remember him," Sharon says as she clears the dishes. Then she pulls ice cream from the refrigerator.

"My mother doesn't like to talk about my father around my stepfather. She's afraid saying anything about my father, her first love, would threaten John, which is ridiculous. Or it's an easy excuse for not telling the truth."

"Maybe she's hiding something. I've learned from my research that nearly every family has at least one secret." She places a plate of store-bought cookies and two bowls of chocolate ice cream on the table.

"But your research is suicide." This remark causes a break in the conversation with the two sitting and eating in silence.

Finally, Cass speaks. "She might be keeping a secret. Adrienne and I weren't allowed to go to the funeral in London, and we both wonder why."

"Children didn't go to funerals in those days. Thank goodness we've changed that attitude. Children need to accept death, especially if it's of a parent. They won't grieve properly if they don't take part in the ceremony."

As a reply, Cass takes the newspaper from the counter and reads aloud the films that are playing.

October 6, 1943

Still in Lucera school — so many deaths from recent casualties, while others bury them have time to write in diary — visit with others here.

Good to be inside, away from cold — cooks like it too — set up better kitchen in classroom than when in field — has running water — cook somehow got ham and a caciocavallo cheese, shaped like a bell — made delicious cheese sauce for spaghetti shaped like shells to go with ham — lemon pie for dessert — soldiers happy after delicious dinner — hard to make dying soldiers comfortable without mattresses, pillows — no linens — everything lice infested — remember laundry day at home — maid would use angle iron on sheets, change beds — clean linen smelled fresh.

No letter from Gloria yet — will write again today telling her I love her — say she should get apartment, make nest for us for after war — shopping for furniture, curtains might cheer her — will write father and ask him to give her more money.

EIGHT

Adrienne

When she finally puts Sam on the plane to North Bay, Adrienne welcomes the solitude. She gets home, and her phone rings. From downstairs, she hears her bedroom machine answer. Tony's tenor voice is barely heard from the living room, but instead of rushing for the kitchen extension, she listens, savouring this quiet. Tonight, she'll see him, but first she'll read today's letter from Aunt Margaret.

March 21, 1995

Dear Adrienne,

I was sorry to hear about your job because I know how you loved working, as did I. Before retiring, I'd work late then go home and cook an egg. As I lived alone, there was no meal prepared or no one for whom to cook, so I ate what was easy. If I'd known sooner, you could have visited me. As it is, next week I'm going with friends to California on a little-old-lady tour. We'll visit Disneyland, MGM Studios, play bridge, and enjoy tasting their wines.

I'm glad you appreciated those letters. Besides writing what I knew on the photo backs, I barely glanced through them. Who knows what you'll find. Maybe some secrets my parents hoped died with them. They were like that: cool, circumspect, and rather shut out of ordinary life.

If your father had lived, your mother and I could have been the friends we were as youngsters. Although she grew up in London, we were only close for a short time. Her parents belonged to a different circle than mine. They had less money but more substance and the same proper stiffness as my parents, which your mother inherited.

The last time I saw her, you were thirteen. She brought you to London after your father died. It was hot, and we sat in the garden. My mother hurt your mother's feelings, which often happened. Your mother never came back, and my mother discouraged me from contacting her. By the time your mother remarried, we hadn't spoken in years. To write or call her now would be difficult.

As children, Alex and I spent time at the Ingersoll farm. I'd cook with the women, and Alex would drive the tractor. We heard wonderful stories. Our grandparents were churchgoers, but farm life was still more fun than London.

The money our father made in hardware changed him. He took over mother's china store and controlled the money that her grandparents made in cigars and her father made in real estate development near Petrolia. After father built the big house, mother strove to raise our social status. She held elegant teas and dinner parties. I shouldn't complain though; I've never had to worry about money, and the education they gave me kept me entertained.

Please come and visit me soon. We can talk more about your father.
Love, Aunt Margaret

This letter makes Adrienne feel close to Margaret because of their mutual fondness for working, which she didn't expect. She's fascinated by the images her aunt paints of her family's businesses — a china store, cigars, and real estate development — and she wants to find out more about these people, the buildings the businesses inhabited, and, in particular, the "big house." Prompted by her desire to know more, she considers visiting London and its surrounding farmland to research them and their lives. Making such a trip would also allow her to reconnect with her aunt.

Obviously, Margaret hadn't considered her father's words about how he couldn't "stop thinking about the dead," or she would have mentioned them. And it's certainly too bad her mother and

Margaret are estranged; they could have been friends. It's interesting to read how Adrienne's grandfather got control of his wife's assets, but from experience, she knows how money can cause conflicts. When Graham lost his investments in the '87 crash, he asked Adrienne for some of her money to invest. Thinking he would lose that too, she refused, and he left. A wave of sadness washes over her when she thinks of Graham and why they divorced. Should she have loaned him money? Would he have taken her advice about investing it? If she had given him money, would they still be together? Would they have any children? She'd probably judged him too harshly, and if she'd been more generous, would that have saved her marriage? Thinking about this possibility makes her sadder.

Needing to forget her failed marriage, she retrieves the lone bottle of Glenfiddich from the liquor cabinet and decides to have a small glass. She sits in the living room and takes sips of the golden liquid, letting a warm flush spread from the soles of her feet to the tips of her fingers. She is enjoying the restful seclusion when, suddenly, the doorbell rings. Her inclination is to ignore it, but it rings again. Through the hall window, she sees Tony on the veranda, dressed for running and holding paper-wrapped flowers.

Once inside, he hands her the bouquet, saying, "I've missed you."

"Me too," she says and pulls his jacket zipper partway down. He draws away.

"I smell alcohol," he says. "Are you drinking by yourself?"

"You sound like my mother, the liquor police. I had enough of her last week."

"Did she drive you to drink?"

"Only wine. She hid the hard stuff."

"Good idea," he says, shaking his head. "I'm telling you up front. I worry about . . . have issues with . . . people who drink alcohol alone. Especially in the middle of the day."

"I drink occasionally. At parties, over dinner, that sort of thing," she says, making points with her index finger. "Socially, I think it's called."

"You're drinking now," he says, his voice more like a high school principal assigning a detention than a policeman. "What's social about doing it alone?"

Adrienne almost says she felt sad, but she knows that would make her sound like an alcoholic, so she chooses "I needed to unwind."

"Go for a jog. Walk around the block. Listen to music," he says and sits on the hall bench.

"I don't have a problem. I just wanted to relax, you know."

"You may not have a problem. But when you drink alone, I do."

"I know you saw that I'd been drinking the day I lost my job. I didn't make a very good impression. And now that you point it out, I realize I haven't really changed my habit much since then." While she's saying this, Adrienne knows that drinking to relieve sadness is reckless, even addictive, behaviour. She vows that starting tomorrow, she'll encourage herself to feel sorrow, without using alcohol to relieve it, even if this means crying to work through the emotion.

"Well, when you do, call me."

"Tony. I didn't mean ..." She watches from the open door while he negotiates the steps. By the time his feet hit the sidewalk, he's running. She shuts the door and rests against it, her heel kicking it repeatedly. Tony, who'd popped into her life unexpectedly, is gone, and she can't deny the physical and emotional attraction she had for him.

Her instinct is to wait a few minutes, then call him. He'll be home soon. Then she'll promise never to drink again. Still, the best idea would be for her to stop drinking, then let him know. Impulsively, she pours the leftover liquid from her glass down the kitchen sink, determined not to cry. She won't get twisted over him. He's just another middle-aged guy, and as her mother says, "There are other fish in the sea." But maybe he's worth it for her to hold out the hook of not drinking to reel him in. But to keep him, she'll have to give up alcohol, and is he worth having to do that?

Adrienne sleeps late the next day and spends the afternoon studying the genealogy book she borrowed from her local library. It tells her how to find the origins of the Muir and MacLean families in Scotland and Ireland, both countries she's always wanted to visit. Now there's nothing stopping her. She should think about going before she gets another job. This borrowed book also tells her the addresses where she can write to find information about her father, like his birth and death certificates. Because she doesn't have envelopes or stamps, she puts these items on her list and tries not to think about Tony and his reaction to her drinking.

After his sudden exit yesterday, she knows they won't be eating together tonight, so she walks to St. Clair, looking for food. Ahead, she sees the Italian place where they first ate together. Basil and tomato mixed with garlic perfume the night air. She decides to eat there and plans that if he turns up, she'll say hello then take her food out. Inside, a family crowds around two pushed-together tables in the centre of the restaurant. Listening to their conversation makes her feel like she has company and reminds her of the discussions her family used to have over Sunday dinner, before her father was drunk by noon. Adrienne and Cass could sometimes get him to talk about popular music, a book he was reading, or the tunes he loved to play on the piano.

The risotto and salad she'd ordered come together. While she eats, she eavesdrops on a man and woman sitting behind her. They're whispering, in delicious detail, about how they'll rush up to their bedroom when they get home, strip naked, and cover each other with kisses. Their talk brings back a time years ago, before her father just sat in his den drinking. Her parents would wash dishes between kisses and murmur Latin phrases to each other in the kitchen. He'd studied it to become a doctor, and she taught it. It was their secret love language that eventually died with his drunkenness. Adrienne suddenly considers how her own drinking might affect, and indeed has affected, the first potentially romantic relationship she's had since Graham left. The first she's taken seriously, but obviously not seriously enough.

The next morning, as Adrienne plans to meet Barb in the den, she begins cleaning it. First, she boots up the old computer to see if it will hold investment software. As it still operates on DOS and has Word Perfect, she orders a new computer and Microsoft Office, which she used at her old firm. When she starts to crave a drink, she decides that for two weeks she'll write "B" in her daybook for when she wants booze. Based on this research, she'll decide whether she has a problem. Until then, she'll have one drink a day before dinner.

Without alcohol to fortify her for the job ahead, she plugs in the kettle and slides bread into the toaster. When the kettle begins to whistle, she's reminded of how this noise has always comforted her. When Adrienne and Cass got older, their mother's kettle would be whistling when they got home from school. The second-best cups, not bone china, and a plate of cookies would sit in the kitchen. When the kettle began its sound, she'd send Adrienne for her father. Sometimes the noise alone brought him down the hall. She and Cass would generously cream and sugar their tea, and their father would taste the tidbits stacked on his saucer. Like an absent-minded professor, his fingers would find some of the buttered bread, cooked meat, and raw vegetables her mother had put on his plate. Often, on his most intoxicated days, tea was his only meal. He'd eat a little then stumble back down the hall to his den.

The computer arrives with a technician who installs the software and the internet service. Soon, documents fly from the file cabinet to a shredding pile. Men from a used furniture store pick up the couch she'd scored from the divorce. When the truck pulls away, all she has left from her marriage is Graham's last name: Adams.

Every day when she craves a drink, she marks "B" in her daybook. Then, she allows herself one scotch before dinner, although it's often very difficult not to have more. By Thursday, the den is nearly bare. She has the rug shampooed and takes the curtains to the cleaners.

Often, she longs for Tony: his height, the way his hair curls, his loud but comfortable laugh, how he smells after jogging, and the way his lips feel on her lips. She reaches for the phone, several times, and dials his number but hangs up at the first ring.

With her astronomy meeting approaching, she goes to the third floor above the streetlights after dinner, hoping to see stars. She writes the date, March 30, 1995, and time, 9:22 p.m., in her log. Very rarely, she can see the brightest stars if she looks north away from the city or west over the park. Tonight, if the urban light pollution doesn't stop her from seeing south, which it usually does, she might find Hydra, the sea serpent, snaking across the sky. Later, in the east, after most of the city's lights are off, she could glimpse Hercules, this serpent's slayer. Stargazing usually prompts the best memories of her father. His drinking never comes to mind when she's looking heavenward. She knows that, if she sees any of these stars tonight, when she reads these log notes to her astronomy club, they'll be impressed.

Long ago, her father had recounted the stars' myths. Now, she looks almost directly overhead with her telescope and waits for her eyes to adjust to the light. There, she imagines seeing Cancer, her sister's astrological sign, signified by the crab. Cass's name, Cassandra, doesn't have a constellation; however, it does appear in Homer. As her father knew Homer, when he saw Cancer in the heavens, he'd reflect that although Cassandra saw the truth, no one believed her prophecies. Adrienne could have reminded her sister of this the other night, but she didn't have the heart. Tonight, to see Hercules, she would have to stay up another hour, and dark skies aren't guaranteed. She'll search for Hercules and Cassiopeia tomorrow, when the club meets at Lucy's on Toronto Island. There, away from city lights, the stars are often visible.

When she wakes the next morning, she's startled by how many "Bs" there are in her daybook. If she'd had a drink each time she wanted one, would she be an alcoholic? At her library, she renews the genealogy book, which she'll need for the letters, and borrows one on substance abuse. Maybe it will give her guidelines to judge her alcohol consumption. She doesn't leave enough time for travelling to the meeting and has to skip dinner. Then, she has to run to make the ferry.

Once at Lucy's yellow and blue cottage, the club members go outside and set up folding stools. Portable telescopes are placed at each spot. Joe is assigned to use his eyes, which sometimes work better than instruments. For the next hour, people rotate and take notes. On the last night in March, from an island in Lake Ontario, Adrienne encounters the Milky Way and remembers it as her father's favourite stargazing sight. A long, luminous path marches from north to south and passes through Cassiopeia, Perseus, and Auriga. Low in the sky looking east is Hercules. And high above, she notes Cass's constellation, Cancer. The brilliance of its cluster, Praesepe, the weather portent, says tomorrow will be clear. She could invite Tony on a walk and point this out, if he ever speaks to her again.

Later, when they're sharing notations at Lucy's, Dell puts up his hand. He compares viewing the Milky Way from the Island to seeing it from downtown Toronto and suggests he write to Toronto Council next week about the light pollution.

"Before you send it, bring it to the next meeting. We'll all sign it," says Adrienne.

"And, Lucy, remember we're meeting at my house next week."

Over the weekend, Adrienne decides to quit pining for Tony and get on with her life, which she's determined will involve learning to control her drinking. She calls Cass to chat, but her sister's voice is so weak that Adrienne thinks she's had a catastrophe.

"What's wrong?"

"I had a dream . . . or maybe a flashback . . . of when Dad almost shot me. But I still can't believe it happened. Besides, Mom said it didn't. Maybe I made it up because of how often you've talked about it. That's what dreams do. But if it did happen, where did the bullet go?"

"It lodged in the baseboard. Made a crack in the plaster wall above it."

"I don't remember," Cass says.

"You wouldn't. Your forgetting is a way to cope," Adrienne says. "A few days after it happened, you and I went to stay at Grandma and Grandpa MacLean's house for a week. When we got back, the bullet had been removed, the crack repaired, and our bedroom was painted pink. Mom probably thought it would make us forget."

"I *do* remember our pink bedroom. After that, I wanted everything pink. Pink dresses, pink socks, even pink library books. I borrowed some uninteresting books to read just because they had pink covers."

"Believe me, it happened. But after he did it, he was crying. He said he was cleaning the gun."

"In the house? Isn't that crazy?"

"Yes. I always thought his behaviour was erratic."

"You might be right. And when I think about that note you showed me. . . about the dead calling him to join them, well the first part of the note interests me too," says Cass. "It said something about him losing his battle fatigue patients."

"Yes, it did," says Adrienne. "Oh my. Now that I think of it, I remember when that happened. Really, he was fired from his job. He came home early that day, looking very upset, but that was nothing to how Mom reacted. She started slamming kitchen cabinet doors and banging pots on the stove. Finally, she said, 'What'll we do for money now?' Dad just turned around and went to the den without saying a word. After that day, he just stayed in there and drank."

"So losing that work was probably a turning point for him," Cass says.

"I remember him telling Mom, once, how he thought his work was important. He was really helping these soldiers get over their memories. When the hospital fired him, he was probably devastated."

"Why did they?"

"I'm not sure. Maybe he was too involved. Maybe the hospital thought he wasn't helping the men. Maybe they thought he was drinking on the job . . . Regardless, his life really changed after that, and I can relate. Losing my job has certainly changed me."

"But you know," says Cass, "the lines in that note about how the dead are calling to him really resonate, too. The thought that maybe he was thinking of suicide also crossed my mind."

"Now you're getting carried away," says Adrienne. "Mom always said he had a heart attack."

"I know, but if he did kill himself, she'd never tell us. We know she's into denial. My friend Sharon, the psychology professor who writes about suicide, says people who have depression, which heavy drinking causes, often kill themselves. Sound like Dad?"

"I know he was depressed," Adrienne says. "I saw it in his eyes, but I'm not ready to say he ever thought about suicide."

Yet the next morning, she goes to the *Globe and Mail* to find her father's obituary.

October 23, 1943

Requested leave at Campobasso, Allied Headquarters — soldiers' playground — Y.M.C.A., Knights of Columbus have canteens there — soldiers dance, drink, play cards, meet women — Grant and I both want to go.

Expect heavy warfare across strait — allies bombed for cover as Americans arrived in Naples — fleeing Jerries destroyed sewer, water systems, which makes day-to-day life very difficult.

Nurses from Catania on leave in Campobasso — rumours one nurse, Velma Miles, asking about me — she's a robust blonde, tells bawdy stories — R.C.A.M.C. might open psychiatric treatment centre — if so, Velma will request transfer — I will too.

Still at Lucera, evacuating casualties to rest camp and filling syringes for heavy fighting. #2 C.I.B. began assault last night — casualties from Carleton Yorks, Edmontons trickling in — Grant knows none of them — I know none from London's Royal Canadian Regiment that are here, so we won't know any dead — hear booms, feel ground shake as war underway — even though won't know them, I dread pain I'll see in men blown limbless, sexless, mindless — men retreat into soul's darkness to escape battle — sometimes I think I'd like to join them.

This war shows no sign of ending. I'm stuck here — will never get home — have to watch men die as I try everything I know — studied hard but still don't have enough medical knowledge to save them — my feelings of sadness and guilt are almost too much to bear.

NINE

ADRIENNE

After searching old microfilm reels at *The Globe and Mail*, Adrienne finally finds her father's obituary.

Dr. Alexander Muir - January 5, 1960

Toronto psychiatrist, Alexander Thomas Muir, died suddenly at home of a heart attack. Born August 14, 1918, in London, Ontario. Son of Hanna and Gordon Muir, husband to Gloria, brother to Margaret, father to Adrienne and Cassandra, received BSc. University of Western Ontario, '39, MD. University of Toronto, '42, served with R.C.A.M.C. first in England then Italy then the liberation of Holland from September 1942 – May 1945. On return, opened General Practice, London, Ont. Later graduated from U. of T., '48, in psychiatry, practiced in Toronto until his death. Service held at St. Paul's Cathedral, London, 11:00 a.m. January 8, 1960, followed by luncheon at the Hunt Club.

The only thing that seems strange here is the invitation for mourners to attend a luncheon at the country club afterward. Yet, from what she knows about her grandmother Muir, Adrienne's not surprised. According to her mother, Alex's parents used any occasion to raise their standing in London society. On the other hand, she knows little about funeral etiquette, so maybe it's common to hold a luncheon for attendees at an upscale club rather than the church hall.

Frustrated by her lack of knowledge about the times in which her parents lived and spurred by this obituary, Adrienne leaves *The Globe* and sets out for the big downtown reference library. Although she usually uses her local library or buys books outright, she hopes this huge collection will yield more information. She knows researching the topics on her list won't give her any precise information about her father's war experience, but the librarians there might be able to tell her where to find it. She'll also learn, among other things, about practicing medicine during WWII. And she's so used to going to work every morning at this time that it seems normal, even emotionally healthy, to finally have somewhere to go.

The subway's rocking lulls her into thinking about how her life has taken a big detour. Today, she's not going to work. Instead, she'll respect the impulse to understand her father's life and hope that seeking this knowledge will cushion the pain she suffers when she thinks about his death. Daily, she settles at a study carrel and reads until one, from books suggested by the librarian, then lunches at a nearby grill, offering only non-alcoholic beverages. This routine reminds her of her university days: a happy, carefree time when she'd use this very library to gain sources only available here. One difference from those days is her upscale clothing, which she enjoys choosing every morning to please herself.

Going home, her back tired from sitting, she gets off the subway one stop early and takes a shortcut through a nearby park. Hyacinth and tulip shoots pepper the earth, and birds chatter from bare trees. As each day passes, her steps lighten, and as her mind fills with WWII knowledge, she thinks less and less about Tony. When he creeps into her thoughts, she dismisses him by considering what living in London, Ontario was like before the war.

She learns how practicing medicine during WWII differed from practicing medicine in a 1940s hospital. With the librarian's help, she finds a list of meanings for military abbreviations. As such initials begin the return addresses of most of her father's letters, suddenly notations like A.D.S., B.D.S., and F.S.U. make sense. She's even able to find pictures of an Advanced Dressing

Station (A.D.S.), a Beach Dressing Station (B.D.S.) and a Field Surgical Unit (F.S.U.). Although she's certain wartime medicine has evolved even since these books were published, she's sure these various stations and units, to this day, would all be housed in hastily erected tents or pre-fab buildings where sutures are applied or amputations performed. At times, care is so urgently required that treatments are performed in the open air, where the sand on a beach could cause enormous sanitary problems. She knows, from childhood memories, the hospitals in London were well equipped, for the time, to perform any required treatment, so the fact that her father operated in crude wartime facilities shows his skill and fills her with pride.

Next, she reads about the history of psychiatry, south-western Ontario farming, and playing golf. Once she understands his world, she wants to know more about her father's day-to-day life: what interested him in school, who taught him piano, and why his parents didn't like her mother. She knows Aunt Margaret is probably the best source for those topics, so she plans on phoning or visiting her for a good chat. One day, she takes the genealogy book she'd first borrowed and the paper, envelopes, and stamps she'd purchased for this purpose to the library, and, after using the addresses of various ministries, writes letters asking for copies of her father's birth, marriage, and death certificates, his will, and his baptismal records. From the book, she also learns how to research her childhood Roxborough home and, most importantly, she discovers that, as a soldier's daughter, she can request copies of his service record. She also finds that the London Public Library has regional family histories, so she writes letters seeking information about the Muir and MacLean families, too. Finally, feeling her research is nearly complete, she returns the genealogy book.

In reality, despite wanting details about the joy and grief that surrounded him, she knows no amount of book research will help her know personal details about her father, just as learning about battles won't tell her about any particular soldier. To find out anything personal about him, she plans to ask Aunt Margaret and her own mother. She knows Aunt Margaret will happily share anything she remembers, but talking to her mother will be difficult.

On the last day she spends at the library, having written all the letters and read what the librarian has offered, she goes home and orders a Margherita pizza, from the restaurant on St. Clair, for dinner. Damp spring air seeps through the walls of her old house, and in search of a sweater, she climbs the stairs to her bedroom. The light on her phone flashes, but she sees *Ringer is Off* in the window. She must have inadvertently turned down the sound and didn't hear the phone ring, yet her answering machine has saved the messages. She puts on a sweater then replays the calls.

"This is Barb Dawson. Jessica sent me a copy of my investment information. Call me."

"Jessica Simpson for Adrienne Adams here. I've been slipping some of your former clients your number. Your stepfather called today and asked questions about why you weren't there. I said as little as possible. Call me for advice on what to say if he or anyone else calls. Bye for now."

"John calling. Your mother wonders why you haven't phoned. We're flying home next week. Get in touch, so you can meet our flight."

"Norman, from astronomy club. I'm sick, and I need to talk to you about finances. Please call as soon as possible."

"Cass here. Number one, your email comes back from your old office account. Get it hooked up at home. Number two: I need to talk to you. Call me."

"Leon Levi reminding you of next Friday's meeting at our house. Rachel looks forward to seeing you. We need to talk about money."

"This is Lucy. I need to talk to you about writing a business plan for the bank. Call me as soon as you can."

Adrienne is pleased that Lucy wants her advice. They'd had lunch at the seafood restaurant near the ferry wharf one Saturday, as planned, to supposedly talk about Adrienne's father's interest in the stars. However, the discussion soon centred on Lucy's parents.

"They emigrated from China before I was born because they thought Canada offered more opportunities," Lucy had said, "but I'm an only child, so all their energy centred on me. They told me where I should go, what I should study, and who I should see. They even insisted I become a teacher."

"Which seems to have worked out," Adrienne said. "From everything you say, I think you like teaching."

"It's okay, except teaching science on this island means we have to go out onto the land and to the shore to make all these discoveries. Everything needs to be hands on to make the most of this place. But it's exhausting taking the children out of the classroom so often."

"Can't you ask to teach a higher grade? That way, the pupils could look after themselves better on field trips."

"And be seen as a complainer? The rest of the staff could make lunch hour unpleasant," Lucy had said. "What I really want to do, rather, what I've always wanted to do, is start a makeup line for women with skin colour like mine."

Adrienne looked at Lucy's face, which she'd always seen as beautiful without makeup. "But you don't use makeup," she'd said. "Why would you start something you don't use?"

"That's the point. I do, but you can't really tell, because it blends with my skin tone," Lucy said. "I made the makeup I use myself. I've made it for years. I just have to figure out how to produce enough of it, to sell it."

"I bet I can help you with that," Adrienne had said, which seemed like a good idea at the time, but now she has to follow up, not just with Lucy, but with all the people who'd called.

When Tony walked away that day, she could have called her mother and sought support, but not wanting to appear needy, she didn't do that. Ironically, now that she's found something to do in her research, everyone needs her, like a child who suddenly starts demanding attention just as her mother decides to return to work. John's calling Jessica is out of character. He usually tries hard, in a reserved but friendly way, to stay out of her life. She goes down to the kitchen and writes *call Barb, John, Norman, Lucy, and Cass* on the erasable board for tomorrow. Leon can wait until next Friday.

As she knows her pizza will arrive shortly, she brews a pot of tea and takes it to the den. There she makes a list of potential business clients then stares out the window at the April night. She's not sure Lucy will become a client, but she's willing to talk to her about what she needs to start a business. Streaks of rain slice through the streetlight's glow. She thinks of her father at war, slogging through the mud, his medical equipment around his neck in the rain, and wonders if it weren't bad enough that he had to go at all. Did he ever write in his journal? If her mother has it, reading what he wrote would be more valuable than anything she might find at the library.

On noticing the time the next morning, she bolts out of bed, concerned by how much more she wants to learn about what her father was dealing with during her childhood. What triggered him from being a reasonably happy, productive doctor to one who no longer practiced and drank all day, alone? She believes it may have been losing his job helping battle fatigue patients. She might never know the answer, especially not before she takes time to job hunt, which frustrates her. It's already the third Friday in April, and she still needs to talk to Aunt Margaret, who she believes has most of the answers.

She's downstairs making coffee when she sees the "call" names on the board. Thankful that Clara cleans on Mondays, she sets appointments with Barb, Norman, Leon, and Lucy, after school, for Tuesday. Then, she calls Florida, praying that John answers.

"Hello," he says in his quiet and quivery eighty-year-old man voice.

"It's Adrienne. You called?"

"Your mother's been worried. She can't figure out why you rushed out of here in March. Wait a minute. I'll get her."

"I'd rather talk to you. I told her why we left. If she needed clarification, she could have called me."

"I've asked her." John's voice is sheepish now. "But she's so busy working at the community kitchen she won't talk. She was glad for a vacation from the soup kitchen in Toronto, but after you left, she started here. It's like she doesn't want to talk to anyone."

"Sounds like Mom. Aunt Margaret gave me a bunch of letters my father wrote home from the war. But Mom won't discuss them in case it upsets you."

"We might have five years left together, if we're lucky," he says, his voice edged with anger. "Her talking about your father won't hurt our relationship, nor would my talking about my internment. It was all so long ago, and we've both had good lives since then. Anyway, we're flying home on Thursday. Can you meet us?"

"I'll check my calendar," she says and holds the phone away, remembering that Monday she's going to the hairdresser's, and Tuesday she's seeing Barb, Norman, Lucy, and Leon. She'll do their paperwork and get them to sign it while they're there, although she thinks Lucy only needs advice. Unless something happens, she's free all-day Thursday.

Pulling the receiver back to her ear she says, "I can't. I'm going to London on Thursday to research my family and meet Aunt Margaret. I've already arranged appointments. My father grew up there, and Aunt Margaret lives there now, too." In reality, she's just told a lie about the appointments she's made, but she doesn't feel like picking them up. It would mean having to talk to her mother politely, which would take too much effort. And it's not like paying for a cab would break them. Besides, she is going to go to London soon, maybe even on Thursday.

"We'll take a cab then. But we should get together . . . about a business idea that might interest you."

Although they've never been as close as a father and daughter might be, she thinks he's worth a listen.

"Okay, but before I devote much time to anything, I want to finish my research."

"When you get back from London, I'll take you to lunch."

Adrienne hangs up the phone and hears the mail slip through the front door slot. A manila envelope from Aunt Margaret yields her father's memorabilia, which Adrienne had sent back to her aunt, wanting answers about each item. There's also a note.

April 1995

Dear Adrienne,

I did the best I could with these items. I have no idea where these letters are from, so my thoughts are mostly conjecture. Regarding the letter about the dead calling your father, it's surprising he didn't say where he was. He was usually precise about the place or hospital a letter was from, so understanding why he seemed very depressed, even hopeless, at the time, might be helped by knowing where he was. Considering these limitations, I could only add what I thought.

Why don't you visit me soon? We could talk more about your father.
Margaret

Her aunt has clipped a paper to each item. On it, she's written her thoughts. Most are letters from Alex when he was young at Hillview, his grandfather's farm, or from university. On the mysterious note, Aunt Margaret has written, *Although he usually wrote in ink and this is pencil, it is Alex's handwriting. It must have been written in October or November, in hospital, the fall before he died.*

Back in the kitchen, Adrienne wonders what Margaret meant in her note about him being hospitalized, and, indeed, what her father meant. She doesn't recall him being sick enough to be in a hospital. She erases Cass's name from the board then picks up the phone and calls her sister in case she remembers something. Before she can ask anything, Cass cheerfully tells her that only two of the courses she teaches have final exams. After she marks those, she's off for the summer.

"Is that what's making you so happy?"

"It's more than that," Cass says and laughs. "I won five thousand dollars in a lottery."

"Hmm," Adrienne says, cautiously. "I thought you weren't buying tickets."

"I bought it before I vowed to stop. This ticket was a fundraiser for the Arts Centre, which I always support. It's ironic that I won with my last lottery ticket!" Cass is suddenly subdued, then finally says, "I think I'm remembering more things about Dad."

In the background, Adrienne hears pots banging and asks if Cass is in the kitchen.

"Sam has a P.D. day. She's learning to make French toast." Faintly, Adrienne hears Sam ask if she should use one egg or two.

"Two. It'll be more nutritious," Cass says, not covering the mouthpiece. Then her quiet voice is back. "I remember. He'd sit in his room for weeks and not go to work. That's probably why he was fired."

"Mom used to say he needed time alone at home to work on difficult cases. For a while, the hospital approved, but finally he was fired."

"And after that, he just stayed in the den and drank. But then I remember, before he died, he went away. Were he and Mom separated?"

Adrienne hears oil sizzling and says, "Sam should turn down the heat."

Cass relays the message, and Adrienne continues, "I don't recall that, but you might have told me the answer. Aunt Margaret says that pencil note from 1959 may have been written while he was in hospital. Now that I think of it, for Halloween he'd dress in something scary and take us out. The fall before he died, we missed Halloween. He was away, and Mom wouldn't take us out. And she wouldn't tell us where he was. He was probably at the hospital drying out . . .you know, getting sober." She stares out the kitchen window from her chair by the phone as the rain, grim and grey as her mood, accumulates on the deck. "I sent Aunt Margaret the note and asked what she thought it meant."

"Why would he write in pencil?"

"Maybe this was a psychiatric hospital, and all they let him have were pencils so he couldn't hurt himself. Of course, this is all speculation because I think either a pen or a pencil could be dangerous."

"He does sound depressed. Maybe his depression really was too much for him, and it killed him like I suspected. I think we should ask Mom."

"You're right. We should."

Adrienne hears muffled voices then Cass says, "According to Sam, John called this morning, worried about Mom."

"He called me too. She claims not to understand why I took Sam to Disneyworld, even though I told her I'd leave if she didn't talk about Dad. That alone says she'll never tell how he died."

"This note helps my memories make sense," Cass says. "He knocked down ice sculptures in a schoolyard, so he certainly had mental health issues. We have to try forcing Mom to talk."

After a long pause Adrienne says, "I don't want to, but I will if we do it together."

"Get your email hooked up so we won't have to spend money on phone calls."

Adrienne strides back and forth in the hall, thinking she's done everything she can to learn about her father. Then she remembers she hasn't read all the letters Aunt Margaret sent, so she goes back to them.

ENGLAND March 8, 1943
#15 G.H.
R.C.A.M.C.

Dear Mother and Father,

I have changed units again and am in a hospital where there's no central heating. It's hard to keep patients warm. Grant Chapman is an M.O. here. Last week we took a refresher course on battle exhaustion, which they called shell shock in W.W.1. We had an air raid this morning, and the ground shook when bombs dropped. Later, two Jerry airmen were admitted. We don't have to like them to save them. They're just soldiers like us, trying to do their jobs. But they will be jailed if they recover. I'm afraid I won't hear about the baby until long after the birth. Please promise you'll find a way to get me the news as quickly as possible.

Love to all, A.

Her father was obviously looking forward to being a father. He also shows his tolerance and dedication to his Hippocratic Oath by working on the German airmen

ENGLAND 13-05-43
#15 G. H.
R.C.A.M.C.

Dear Mr. and Mrs. Muir,

I am writing as Alex's friend. He took the baby's death hard. He was worried about his wife, but he never got the cablegram you claim to have sent and had to wait for your letter. After it came, I ordered him to complete bed rest with extra rations. This is how we treat battle exhaustion. When we're shipped out, Alex will be busier saving men. Then his spirits will improve. Please reassure him that you have seen Gloria, and that she'll be fine.
Yours truly, Dr. G. Chapman

Adrienne finds it fascinating to read how the trauma of losing a baby was treated the same way as battle exhaustion, now known as post-traumatic stress disorder. When she considers it, bed rest and extra rations are similar to taking an all-inclusive vacation, which would relieve anyone's stress.

ENGLAND 07-06-43
#15 G.H.

Dear Mother and Father,

I'm doing inoculations, so we must be going to Africa or the Mediterranean, but we won't know until we get there. This job is to help me get over my sadness, which developed when your letter came, Father. I never got the cablegram. I know Grant Chapman wrote to you, but I am somewhat better now. I would like to hear from Gloria before I go but remind myself not to expect anything. Her grief will make her convalescence longer.
A.

Adrienne stops reading and considers how painful that death must have been for her parents. Losing a child at birth is bad enough, but with her mother and father separated, it would have been even worse. She, who'd hoped for a baby with Graham, can't imagine carrying a child for nine months only to lose it. And then, having no work outside her home to fill the time, her mother's life must have been agonizing. It relieves her to know how concerned and caring her father was, not only about his wife's loss but also his own, while undergoing the trauma of war.

SORTINO, SICILY 12-07-43
5th Cdn Fld Amb
R.C.A.M.C.

Dear Mother,

On the crossing, men were seasick, and ships were hit by torpedoes and sank. By the time we landed, the remaining crafts were filled with vomit, and I had to wrap ankles that were sprained from slipping. The local citizens are hungry and disheartened. There was no mail when we arrived and no hope for any. Today we moved to an olive grove. In this heat, I wear shorts until 1930 and trousers after. I rest from 1130 to 1400 hrs, when possible. At night, I use mosquito repellent and sleep under nets. Hopefully, the officers will be billeted in better quarters soon and I'll get leave. Have Gloria's spirits returned?
Love Alex

The next item is a black-and-white postcard. Two uniformed men stand in front of a hotel canopy.

CATANIA, SICILY August 17, 1943

Dear Mother and Father,

I am on leave here with Grant. The buildings are made of black volcanic rock from nearby erupted mountains. The ocean is beautiful, but the town is dark and ominous. We sleep in clean beds, stay out late, eat seafood, and go to the beach with Canadian

doctors from the hospital here. It's lovely not to have to think about men dying.
A

It's a relief to Adrienne to read that there were some enjoyable moments in her father`s wartime experience. She's also learned, from reading his letters, that facing adversity and living through it can be rewarding. Although the biggest difficulty she's faced recently is losing her job, she knows she's grown by finding a way to get beyond that loss.

CATANZARO, ITALY 13-09-43
5TH Cdn. Fld. Amb.
R.C.A.M.C.

Dear Mother and Father,

We are on the mainland and have moved several times. Blown bridges make progress slow, especially in the rain. On arrival, mail was distributed. My first letter from Gloria since our son died seems incongruous. It was dated in July when we were on the ocean. She said she missed teaching. If she were working, she wouldn't have time to brood about the baby. If you could visit her, you could cheer her by saying we'll have a good life. I'll work hard for her and the children we'll have. And we'll have many.
Love, Alex

MT. PALTAGIROME 30-09-43
5th Cdn Fld Amb
R.C.A.M.C.

Dear Mother and Father,

I haven't heard from Gloria since that last bleak letter. Grant Chapman wrote to her parents after the stillbirth. I wish I would hear she was feeling cheerier.

We are in the mountains where the Jerries buried land mines. Our sappers sometimes miss some, then they explode and injure our

soldiers. One victim, from the Princess Pats, had played football with Grant. I amputated his right leg at the hip and most of his left foot, but he died. After that, I felt hopeless at my inability to help him because of what war did. Grant just shook his head and said, "He sure could run," and there was nothing I could do to relieve Grant's sorrow at the loss of his friend.
A.

A muscle cramps in Adrienne's leg. She springs to her feet, flexing her thigh. Although her watch says 12:30 a.m., she hasn't finished reading his letters. It's after midnight, and her eyes are tired from deciphering his writing, yet her heart is aching at what her father had to endure and how he was repulsed by war. Should anyone ever have to tolerate what he did? She has learned from his letters that he was a sensitive man and wishes she'd had the chance to know him as an adult. To love him as an adult. After sitting with her sadness for several minutes, she goes upstairs and climbs into bed.

She's locking her car in the St. Clair lot when a police cruiser, siren screaming, pulls onto the asphalt four rows over. Obviously, there's been something ugly like a stabbing or shooting. With her head craned sideways at the flashing lights, she walks toward the grocery store. So absorbed she bumps into someone on the sidewalk, trips over a foot, and pitches to the ground. She checks herself for injuries and, still prone, notices her victim's shoes. They're stained, black leather runners. Her eyes slide upward past some nondescript jogging pants to an outstretched hand. Tony's hand. She'd recognize the carefully manicured nails any day.

"I kept hoping I'd run into you," he says, a strong arm pulling her to her feet. "No pun intended of course." He pulls her upright and she drops his hand and brushes bits of gravel from her pants. Next to her, crates of red and yellow onions scent the air.

"I'm sorry. I was more interested in the crime scene than where I was going," she says, trying to sound light.

"I wasn't watching either. There's a cafe up the street. Should we have coffee and discuss who's suing whom?"

Since he last walked out her door, she's often rehearsed what she'd say if she saw him, but her carefully constructed phrases have vanished.

"No thanks. Don't pretend you didn't leave without even a look back."

"I almost called you several times . . . to explain." He shoves his hands into his pockets. "Once, I even let the phone ring."

"What's to explain?"

"You're right . . . at least have coffee with me." He reaches out to touch her arm.

"Coffee's not on my list for today," she says and turns toward the store. She's taken several steps when she decides she doesn't want to end all hope for this relationship, so she turns around and walks toward him, smiling.

"When could I see you?" he asks.

"Call me again, and let it ring long enough so you can leave a message."

Inside the supermarket, she sits on the window ledge, her legs trembling, and watches him jog away. Yanking a cart from its metal chain, she starts filling it with apples, asparagus, and parsley. She realizes, in front of the spaghetti squash, that she's added several items not on her list. If he calls this afternoon with a sensible explanation, she'll invite him for dinner. Hopefully, that will encourage him to stay interested in her.

Adrienne feels restless all afternoon, and the fact that she's thinking about Tony while drinking too much coffee doesn't help. She should phone Aunt Margaret and check that she'll be in London on Thursday, so Adrienne can go for a visit, but once in the kitchen, she dials Tony's number and hangs up before it rings. She should have had coffee with him. Maybe what he has to say is simple, even excusable. She eats dinner and hopes he'll call or drop by and beg her to take him back.

With the dishwasher loaded, she fills her thermos with camomile tea and puts several double-chocolate fudge cookies on a plate. Not taking the whole box makes her feel virtuous. She locks the doors, goes up to her observatory, and sets the plate near her telescope. Her log sits open on her desk. After writing today's date — Saturday, April 22, 1995 — in the book, she puts the thermos and the cookies on the table and tips the scope upward to look straight overhead.

Sometimes, if she's patient, she can see through the light haze covering Toronto and into the sky's darkest area. Tonight, she imagines seeing parts of Leo, a lion ready to pounce. Only two stars of six in the sickle symbolizing his head are visible, and only barely. One is Regulus, Latin for 'little king', representing Leo's heart. According to myth, Leo is the Nemean Lion's soul. This is all she can remember about the story. If she ever has any children, she'll relearn these tales, so her kids can enjoy hearing them and know about her father.

She remembers how, when she was four or five and first able to watch the night skies with him, he'd tell his own version of Hercules skinning the lion. In his account, Hercules was as tall as a totem pole and as wide as an elephant, with claws as sharp as a sword that could cut through metal. Hercules lured the lion back into his cave by tripping him with giant feet, and that is as much as she can remember about her father's adaptation. It's as if she wants to dismiss his imagination as flawed, yet she knows he was trying to teach her about perseverance, a characteristic she's used all her life, despite adversity. Her father seemed unable to persevere at the end, giving in to the drink in his hand. Yet, now that she's read about some of the horrendous things he endured, and the memories that obviously plagued him, she can understand his need to block them out with alcohol. The loss of her job hardly compares to the trauma he underwent, so she shouldn't find her drinking acceptable.

She eats cookies and enters her imagined sighting of Leo in her log. As fudge filling smudges across the blue lined paper, she tears the smeared page out of its spiral binding and begins recopying to preserve her stargazing history. On hearing the intercom bell ring in the upstairs hallway, her chest quivers. This is not Tony, she cautions. He'd never come after ten. Who then? The police with bad news?

Expecting an emergency, she presses the speaker button and asks, "Who's there?"

"It's Tony. I thought if you're still up, maybe we could talk."

"Wait there. I'll come down." She's on the second-floor landing before she realizes she's running and hopes he can't hear the anticipation in her pounding feet. Slowing to catch her breath, she sees she's forgotten to turn on the porch light. To make sure it's him, she presses the buzzer for the front hall's intercom system.

"How do I know you're Tony?"

"I'm wearing black leather running shoes and splash pants."

"How do I know you won't say or do something that hurts me again?"

"I already have a few times. Once I walked out without any explanation. I'm here to give that now. And today I knocked you down in the grocery store parking lot. If I were you, I wouldn't answer the door, but if you'd let me install sensor lights out here, you could see me when I stop by at night."

She opens the door and asks, "How soon can you get that done?"

"I'll send someone over on Monday," he says, reaching out to hug her.

She leans forward and puts her hands on his shoulders, feigning a hug. Gesturing for him to enter, she says, "Late Monday is okay. Otherwise, Wednesday. I've got clients coming, and I don't want to have to stop and give instructions."

"Are you back in business?" he asks and wipes his feet on the mat.

"Just a few friends who need help with their money."

She hesitates about how far in she wants him to come. Without offering to take his coat, she sits on the hall's bench. Then, she half-heartedly pats the space next to her.

"I think I'll stand. After I finish, you might want me to leave."

He shoves his hands in his pockets and begins with his father, a Sudbury miner who drank on the weekends, then worked during the week to keep food on the table.

"He'd rough me up unless I stayed out of his way. On the weekends, my mother would worry about my father . . . getting home safely. Then when he did, he'd yell at her until he passed out."

Tony keeps talking, and Adrienne wonders when he'll finish. He says that when he graduated from high school, he went to Police College, then the O.P.P. hired him. It seemed like a safe place to work. His father didn't mess much with police, so Tony thought he wouldn't be found. Later, he applied to Toronto's city police because he wanted to live as far away from home as his work could take him.

"So I could be anonymous — where no one knew anything about me."

He continues with how, while investigating a bomb threat at a school during his first month at work, he met his future wife. His hands are still in his pockets. Where this stance might make other men look vulnerable, he seems at ease, telling his life's story.

He takes a hand from his pocket to rub his forehead and says, "I'd never met anyone like Amber. She was a kindergarten teacher who loved children. But after the wedding, I started being angry. About everything."

Although Adrienne has wanted, more than anything, to ask about his wife, she gasps then to cover it up. She asks, "What do you mean?"

"I started to act like my father, drinking and staying out late." He looks down at his feet. "To stay married, I needed help. Luckily, I found a good psychologist. By the time my sons were big enough for t-ball, I was grown-up enough to coach them."

"You mean, you became what your father wasn't — sober, patient, and loving?"

He nods and keeps talking. He tells how Amber got sick with scleroderma, a little-known autoimmune disease, after the boys were in school. She'd returned to teaching, but she only lived a year after it was diagnosed.

"I'm so sorry. How did you manage?"

"Badly at first, but the police force gave me leave. Then, I took the night shift, so I'd be there for breakfast and after school. I'd sleep when they were in class. I found someone to stay with the boys at night. We learned to clean, cook, and do laundry, and I taught them to swim, and hike, and camp, all of which you and I could do together, if you're interested."

He's taking short, shallow breaths now, as if he just finished a marathon. Then, he shifts his weight backward. Both hands clutch the air for balance. She grabs one to steady him, and he inadvertently pulls her toward him. He turns and sits on the bench.

"Every time I tell this story, I swear I'm over it."

"Who'd ever get over something like that?"

"After a while, I thought about finding someone." He straightens his back. "But everyone I've met had some issue."

When Adrienne raises her eyebrows as if to question his meaning, Tony says, "You know, like obsessive compulsive disorder, or anorexia, or narcissism. And I'd rather be alone than cope with a drinker. I hope you can understand."

"If we were seeing each other, I could because my father was a drinker. I know what that did to my family. But we're not. Besides, you've just dumped new information on me, like your sons. I know we've only known each other a few months, but you could have told me about them. You never bothered . . ."

"They're grown and self-sufficient," he says, hands resting at his thighs. "One is an engineer in Texas. The other teaches high school history here, in Toronto." Laughing, he adds, "I'm nowhere near the *Guinness Book of World Records'* youngest dad in age, but I certainly had a lot of growing up to do . . . emotionally . . . after I became a father."

"If I'd started early, I could have adult children, but I wouldn't keep them secret."

"Protecting them was all I ever cared about. Part of that was not talking about them."

"Well, I've never told you I was married once," she says, touching his shoulder. "I didn't want to scare you off."

"Your drinking scared me enough."

"Me too. I started keeping track of when I wanted it. Turned out . . . it was too often. Once in a while now, I have a drink before dinner. That's it."

She's not going to say she gave it up for him. Not now . . . not yet.

Adrienne wants to know how his grandparents, who left Naples for Canada to escape its poverty and crime, produced a brute like Tony's father.

When she can't find suitable words, she says, "Tell me about your mother."

"The only thing you need to know is she picked the wrong man to marry, and my grandparents knew it."

This statement takes Adrienne by surprise. Suddenly, she knows that she'd made the same mistake when she married Graham, but her mother didn't know it. He'd charmed her with his good looks and grandiose plans. She believed he was a good match for Adrienne because he was in her field, and they'd always have things in common. She was married to Graham before her mother married John, so he didn't get to know Graham before Adrienne married him. If he had, John would have seen through Graham and how he often coloured the truth, and he would have found a way to tell her that didn't offend her.

For a long time, she and Tony sit side by side in silence on the bench, each in thought. Then, he puts his arm around her. Soon they rest their heads together, skull touching skull.

"You don't have some estranged husband lurking around, do you?"

She has time to shake her head once before he kisses her. Soon, they're on the front-hall rug undoing each other's buttons. Tony, who's still wearing his jacket, keeps sliding backwards toward the bench. She reaches under the waistband of his sweatpants to pull out his shirttail, and he shifts his body upward to help. His head cracks against the seat.

"Ouch," he says and rubs the back of his head.

"Are you okay?"

"I'm too old to roll around on the floor. Besides, I just ran three miles . . . I need a shower."

She stands up and extends her hand. Safely upright, he rubs

the bump on his head then lifts her hand to his lips.

"Basically, I prefer to take these things slowly. I'm going home now. Let's go to brunch tomorrow, spend the day together. See what develops."

"Or we could have dinner here, you know . . . more intimate?"

"Sure," he says, his face brightening to a smile. "I'll bring dessert. Six o'clock okay?"

When she nods, he zips up his jacket, brushes her lips with his, opens the door, and runs down the steps into the night.

She gets up Sunday morning, pretending Tony eats and sleeps here every day, and decides she won't worry about dinner until late this afternoon when she'll order it in. That way, her day won't be spoiled by worry about cooking something special for dinner. Instead, she'll read the last of her father's letters.

In the 1970s, while working for the bank, she'd met young men whose lives were forever changed by the Vietnam War. Some were US soldiers who'd fought but deserted to Toronto as soon as they returned home. Others were war resisters who'd sought asylum in Canada. At the time, they'd carried with them a certain mystique that condemned all combat. Now, she seeks that denunciation in her father's experience, hoping to make the sadness these letters produce in her more bearable.

The letter that's made her saddest, so far, is the one where her father had to amputate the leg and foot of a football friend of Grant's. He died anyway. Adrienne finally understands that a doctor who'd sworn to do no harm would be shattered, emotionally, at not being able to save men. She's certain the more letters she reads, the more sympathy she'll have for her father and all he had to suffer in the name of war.

LUCERA 31-10-43
5th Cdn Fld Amb.
R.C.A.M.C

Dear Mother and Father,

The cases I see demoralize me. One, a woman Grandma Muir's age, was hit by a grenade. Everything she said had to be interpreted. I amputated her arm near the shoulder and her leg below the knee. After surgery, she asked how she would work. I knew she'd be a burden to her family, but despite her injuries, I had a duty to save her just as I must save all those I can.

The bridges are impassable over rain-swollen rivers. Ambulance cars slide into ditches, so we have mules carrying the wounded. Casualties die waiting to be transported, or they catch hepatitis. There is nothing glorious about war.
A.

Tears fill her eyes as Adrienne reads this letter. It's almost unbearable to think about her father having to deny this woman her ability to support her family just to save her. What would having to make these life-and-death decisions, day after day, do to anyone's psyche? Great damage, she thinks, and she's certain that's what it did to her father.

ROCCA SAN GIOVANNI 16-12-43
5th Can Fld Amb.
R.C.A.M.C.

Dear Mother and Father,

Aerograms are in short supply, so I stole this one from a dead man. Gloria wants a divorce. She says we didn't know each other well enough when we married, and she wants to teach. I wrote that I don't need this worry now. We are close to the front. Bloated bodies float down the river, and bombardment goes on all night, resulting in many casualties. Soldiers need gruesome operations, after which they die. Our latrine diggers dig graves. Several soldiers have been sent to a small psychiatric unit across the way. Before they're sedated, their screaming pierces the pandemonium. There are many neuropsychiatric patients as a result of this war, and we concentrate on them as well as surgical cases. Treatment results are dismal.

An Edmonton Platoon was wiped out by treachery. The Jerries pretended to surrender, then opened fire. I know that what we're doing is right, but when I see the broken, bloody bodies of young men, I wonder if winning is worth all this.
A.

After reading this letter, Adrienne wonders whether she can stand to read the rest. Her empathy for her father and the necessity that he had to keep working to save these soldiers, rather than walking away, is overwhelming. Suddenly, she remembers him laughing at a funny passage from one of the books he read her, and she wishes she'd spent more time with him in his den, trying to understand him and his war experience. To ease her guilt, she tells herself he'd stopped talking and started drinking too soon.

ORTONA 22-12-43
5th Can Fld Amb.
R.C.A.M.C.

Dear Father,

I am here at a RAP, close to the battle. The noise of jeeps grinding by is tremendous, and the wounded arrive continuously. The stench of death is everywhere — on my clothes, in my hair, on the bandages and bedding. I can no longer count how many men have died today, all brave men who fought their way to heaven. The slime of their blood and mud cover my boots, and grief for them numbs me. I have not washed in days and have no time to eat but must keep going. I hear stories of men hiding in churches which the Jerries blow up. Both sides have savaged the sacred in the name of war. Nothing prepared me for this.
A.

At his mention of the sacred, Adrienne wonders whether her father prayed during this battle of Ortona. She knows from her library research that this conflict was a crucial win for Canadian troops.

ORTONA 26-12-43
5th Can Fld Amb.
R.C.A.M.C.

Mother,

I cannot write the horrors. I've seen rivers of blood running in the streets and women flattened by tanks and their guts spread onto the cobblestones and left for the birds. Some are brought to me for repairs with no life left in them. The killing goes on and on and on and on and the dead are everywhere. Besides the casualties and the corpses, I cannot stand the lice and fleas and noise and smoke and dirt and stench anymore, but there is nowhere to hide and nothing to do but bear it.

A.

Again and again during the day, her face wet, Adrienne rereads the last four letters so eloquently written by a man worn out by war. The fighting continued for more than a year after the last aerogram's date. Perhaps some of the undated letters were written after that, or maybe her father didn't stay until the end. The National Archives' War Diaries will tell her that. Adrienne is shocked to read that while her father was dealing, every day, with so many appalling things, her mother wanted a divorce. It would have added to his feeling of abandonment that war forced on him. In her childhood, the only sign of strain between her parents was the odd time her mother slept on a cot in her sewing room. And Adrienne knows from experience that those times occur even in happy relationships.

She dusts the lived-in areas of the house, in case Tony wants a tour, then goes to the kitchen and gets out the good dishes. After stripping her bed and changing the sheets, she puts fresh towels in the bathroom. Satisfied that the house is presentable, she goes back to reread the last several letters from Ortona. Again, she wonders how long she'd tolerate people dying all around her, smoke, noise, and stench everywhere, sleeping with lice, and repairing every ruined body that came to her. Not long, she thought, not long . . . At four-thirty, she convinces the restaurant on St. Clair, where she and Tony first ate, to send two orders of eggplant parmesan, that day's risotto, and a salad by cab. She scrubs and polishes every inch of her body, finger and toenails included, and dresses in a black, deeply V-necked shirt and elastic-waisted skirt, for easy removal. After Tony arrives, the food sits on the counter while they listen to a new CD he brought. He persuades her to dance. For the next while, they concentrate on touching in the way lovers do.

She takes his hand and starts toward the bedroom when he says, "There'll be time later. Let's eat."

He gets bottled water from the fridge, where he's stuck his strawberry mousse, and, tipping it toward her like a wine steward, says, "Shall I decant this?"

"That would be lovely."

Pointing to some crystal in the glass-fronted cupboard, she remembers how she'd suspected John of paying Tony to spy on her. Now, she'll judge whether his lovemaking is worth the drinking she's had to give up to reach this point.

On their way to her bedroom after dinner, they stop several times to explore each other, at first cautiously through their clothes, then urgently. When they're familiar enough to undo every button, their exploring becomes more adventurous: he with his mouth, she with her hands, until he enters her, at first tentatively and then boldly, over and over, all the while fondling her breasts. Finally, pleasure spreads throughout her body, like a stream springing from its source and rushing to the sea. When they're both exhausted, Tony falls asleep, sprawled naked on her top sheet. Adrienne drifts off, enjoying the sight of him and contemplating the wonder of her climaxing on their first try.

The next morning, sticky and covered with dried sweat and semen, they shower together, which takes more time and is more pleasurable than she'd imagined. They make and eat breakfast together, then Tony slips into the loafers he wore to dinner and says, "I'll send someone over to install the sensor lights about three this afternoon. Then tonight, I'll come and inspect the job myself."

She sifts through the mail and waits for the man Tony is sending to install the lights. Her bank statement shows more order in her finances, but the other mail is solicitations. She's about to toss them when she notices a small, hand-addressed envelope from Aunt Margaret. Inside it is a brief note.

London, Ontario
April 23, 1995

Dear Adrienne,

Before you start working again, you should come for a visit. Please remember to call ahead, as I'm often out of my room at some activity or away on a trip. When you come, bring your address book so I can get your mother's and Cass's addresses. I want to invite you all to a Muir reunion Rose and I are having July 1st. Canada Day falls on a long weekend this year, and now that we've resumed our relationship, we thought we'd celebrate with an old-fashioned picnic. Love, Margaret

This heartwarming invitation suggests that she should visit London on Thursday, but she must call ahead and check that Margaret will be there. Just as she picks up the phone to do that, Tony turns up at her door. He checks the lights by standing in several locations inside, to confirm porch visibility.

"Now, if some reprobate like me rings your bell, you'll be able to see him and not answer the door."

"Show me the reprobate in you," she says and kisses him. Soon they're touching each other again, and, as if he's been planning this all afternoon, he begins to undress her, which leads to another lovemaking session. Later, as they're reassembling their clothes, the phone rings.

"Let it go," he says, pulling her close. "They'll try again."

But she leaves her jeans on the floor and hurries to the kitchen saying, "I'll bet that's Cass. I told her to call if she remembers something about our father. I'm sorry . . . I don't want to stop, Tony, but I need to talk to my sister."

He shrugs and pulls away, his face dark with disappointment.

Over her "Hello," Adrienne hears Cass sobbing. Between gasps she says, "I've been thinking more and more about his note on battle fatigue patients and how losing them changed his life. I think we have to consider the possibility that he killed himself."

"Although I've wanted to believe it was a heart attack," Adrienne says, coming close to tears herself, "you're probably right. Today, I finished reading his letters. Near the end of the war, he wrote about how terrible the fighting was and how he couldn't fix the soldiers. It's obvious the war changed him, and not for the better. The killing nearly drove him mad . . . or maybe it did. I'm sorry I ever judged him for drinking and wish that I'd spent more time with him, showed him more respect for going to war. And more than anything, I'd like to have the chance to give him one last hug."

Cass has stopped sobbing and says, "Maybe he did it while you were at piano lessons."

"Could be. By the time I got home the ambulance had taken him, Mom didn't want us to go into his den. I wonder . . . "

Then Tony comes to the kitchen door, her jeans in his outstretched hand. She slips into them without speaking and goes back to talking with Cass.

"It's horrible to think about. Maybe Margaret knows. I'm going to London on Thursday. I'll talk to her, then I'll call you. We'll figure out how to ask Mom. I'd like her to tell us without having to harass her. She might stop denying things and opt for the truth."

After she hangs up the phone, Adrienne finds Tony sitting on the couch in the living room, looking dejected.

"I'm sorry I had to answer the phone. I want to get back to where we were, but I need to ask your opinion, as a policeman, about my father's death."

He nods, his face lighting a little, and says, "Go ahead."

She briefly describes what she believes was her father's

depression, fuelled by alcohol, before his death. Then she recites the note that's kept her wondering and follows it with "My mother always maintained he had a heart attack. Do you think he could have committed suicide?"

"It certainly sounds like he was thinking about it."

"In that case, based on your conjecture and my gut feeling, I think my father killed himself."

December 9, 1943

Haven't written in diary for weeks — didn't get to Campobasso — got November leave in Naples — saw friends, drank, danced — had smashing time with Velma Miles, who was there on way to Caserta Psychiatric Centre.

5th Field Amb. first unit open for fighting on Sangro/Moro River fronts — we're in Municipio — chapel and badly-damaged church — bridges impassable — casualties evacuated by rivers — Major Doyle the psychiatrist has too many patients so moved.

Bombardment from assault across Moro heard in Rome — continued for 48 hours, don't know when will end — all M.O's operate on wounded — steady barrage exhausts us, take drugs to stay awake — two #1 Can. F.D.S. M.Os came to help as most of our M.O's under psychiatric care.

More gas gangrene cases so increasing serum units — weren't told about serum until too late, so gangrene left yesterday's cases inoperable — not enough morphine so died in agony.

Applied for transfer to Caserta — still with 5th Field — Lieutenant MacLean nearby with Seaforths — may be related to Gloria — fine soldier, be proud to call him cousin-in-law if Gloria and I still married when I get home — if I ever do.

TEN

Gloria

As John gets ready for bed, Gloria asks, "Why didn't Adrienne come to the airport?"

"She knew I could manage a cab," he says and buttons the blue-striped pyjamas she bought him in Florida. "Besides, I'm not sure she wants to see you."

She sits on the bed, her back to him. Finally, she says, "I don't know why."

"Adrienne went to Florida to talk to you about her father. She says you wouldn't talk because you thought it would hurt our marriage. I told her nothing you said would cause trouble between us."

"I don't know what she wants," Gloria says, sounding exasperated. "He was a psychiatrist in Toronto, who worked at a hospital. One day when Adrienne was at piano lessons . . . he died."

"She says she wants to hear about his boyhood, his parents, that sort of thing."

"I've told her before. I don't know much. I don't know if anyone does, unless it's Margaret. Adrienne's going to London; she should ask her aunt. Maybe then her cross-examination will stop." She kisses her finger and puts it to his lips, saying, "I'm tired. Let's talk in the morning."

"I'm tired too, but this talk isn't over."

She slides down between the sheets, the duvet under her chin, and stares at the ceiling. Her brain is racing, so she tries to calm herself by taking deep relaxing breaths. When that doesn't work, she recites several nursery rhymes in her head, but her mind won't stop. Above all, she wants to avoid thinking about Alex. She's almost managed, over the years, to eradicate him from her memory, but recently, Adrienne's questions have put him front and centre, where he continues to drift across the surface of her mind like angry whitecaps on a lake.

Often, she recalls him at the station near his army training camp as she prepares to return to London, his hand outstretched in a wave. Their honeymoon over, he is awaiting orders. As if all he needed to survive a war intact was a smartly pressed uniform. When she sees him there, he's the honest, straightforward man she married, his handsome features lit by their honeymoon's passion. She'd never met anyone who did and said exactly what he believed. Compared to her stuffy relatives, including both his and her parents, he was a fresh breeze. Until war interfered. She's come to understand that those early months were the happiest in their marriage.

Desperate for sleep, she keeps reliving the day, more than a half-century ago, when her parents received the letter from the front about Alex and what she came to consider his condition. She'd fallen into gloom after the stillbirth and confined herself to her bedroom for several months. One afternoon, her parents came to her door and begged her to have tea. Her mother had baked a raisin scone; Gloria can still see the sugar crystals glistening on the round, browned biscuit. There was whipped cream, a rare luxury, so she should have known there was purpose in this preparation. Her father, Duncan MacLean, overly tall with a clean-shaven face and brush of thick black hair, lead her to the dining room table, laid for tea. Gesturing for her to sit, he took his armchair from its head-of-the-table position and, placing it next to her, sat down. Her mother stood behind him.

After withdrawing an airmail envelope from his suit jacket, he removed some blue onionskin sheets from it and began to read. The letter was from Grant Chapman, an M.O. colleague of Alex's. Odd she remembered his name after more than fifty years.

He described Alex, who was being treated for "battle exhaustion," as taking the news of their baby's death hard. According to Grant, Gloria should write and say she was improving, and they would have another baby when he got home. As he read the letter aloud, her father's reserved face took on a disapproving look. She smiles now, remembering that even such an oblique reference to sex made him uneasy. He thought Alex's response to the baby's death might signal a character weakness. After all, a man shouldn't let his emotions affect his performance at war. Alex was there to save lives, and any personal tragedy should be handled without fuss.

"Maybe he's unstable," her mother said.

"More like godless," her father said. "But you're married now. You'll have to make the best of it."

As if it were planned, her mother went to the kitchen while her father finished his point. Although he'd disapproved of Alex's family from the beginning — their money squandering, smoking, drinking, and belonging to the Hunt Club — he thought it was time Gloria went to live at her in-laws' house. She'd lost their grandchild, and his parents did have some responsibility for her. Besides, Hanna Muir had called on them recently and made the suggestion. Since Margaret was getting her own apartment, there would be room, and Gloria wouldn't have to cook, clean, or iron at the Muirs'. They had help.

She didn't know Alex's parents well, but what she knew intimidated her. Their names, Hanna and Gordon Muir, appeared regularly in the newspaper's social column. In Hanna's presence, Gloria felt clumsy. Her mother-in-law was a woman with an antique-silver veneer whose clothes came from Toronto. Gordon, who wore imported business suits while weighing nails in his hardware store, was overbearing, authoritarian, and 180 degrees from his father, Oliver Muir — a generous, thoughtful man with whom she'd boarded while teaching in Ingersoll. She was fond of Margaret, Alex's sister, but Margaret would be off in her own apartment.

The thought of moving to the Muirs' made her cry, and she

ran from the room. While she was sequestered in her bedroom, no one brought her dinner, and her mother, who usually checked on her, stayed away. Gloria felt abandoned. With hours alone to consider her life, she planned what she'd do. She'd married Alex before she was ready, gone to Nova Scotia on the army's orders, gotten pregnant, and lost their son. She pined for the years she'd spent working and in control of her own money, her life. But the Muirs objected to her teaching, for appearances' sake. Gloria realized if she were single, she could find a job. She'd saved what Alex sent home for an apartment, so she had money. Without stopping to consider it, she wrote Alex and suggested they end their marriage.

The next morning, she bathed, put on her best business dress, and took the letter to the post office. On her way home, she stopped at her parents' church and spoke with the minister. He'd come from Toronto since the war started. Although she'd heard her father grumble about his modern ways, Gloria hoped he'd be supportive. That day, the minister's face unemotional, he warned that proven adultery was the only grounds for divorce in Canada, unless one of the participants could be proven to have been incompetent at the time of the ceremony. He lectured her about burdening a soldier with such worries. Then, with a wink, he said she'd feel better once Alex came home and they worked on another baby. She knew then that her only choice was to stay married, yet she went home and told her parents she'd asked Alex for a divorce. She said, to maintain appearances, she'd relinquish her plans for freedom on one condition: they let her live with them until Alex returned.

In a mood like the forest at midnight, Gloria watches her bedroom lighten. She's spent the last eight hours in intermittent sleep, obsessed with a man who's been dead for thirty-five years. When she thinks of him now, in daylight, she knows that his war experience set him on a path to self-destruction, and what he became and how it affected his marriage was far from what she expected when they fell in love and married. Although living with his depression and drinking made her question, at times, how long she could put up with his behaviour, she never stopped loving him for as long as he was alive.

In the long view, it might have been easier on her to divorce him, but that would have destroyed him and any hope she had of his rehabilitation. Of course, in those days, she'd have had to prove he was an adulterer, something she suspected of him during the war, but getting a friend of Alex's or Velma Miles to testify to that would have been impossible. During war, the participants always stuck together, for survival.

Abruptly, she relives a scene in her Roxborough kitchen when Alex teased Cass about her name.

"What did my little Cassandra do today?" he asked, his voice elated, before he became despondent and began sitting in his den all day every day.

"The boys wouldn't let me play baseball at recess," Cass said, a child of about seven at the time. "So I told my teacher."

"I bet she thought you were tattling," Alex said and lifted his tea cup in salute. "That's what Cassandra means. Like reconnaissance men, or the Oracle at Delphi, you foresee the apocalypse but aren't believed."

"That's yucky. I didn't see a pot-of-lips. I wanted to play," said Cass, her face crumpling.

"I meant that men don't like to hear the truth."

Cass looked down at her apron and said, "I told the truth like you taught me."

Gloria is certain that Cass has forgotten that discussion, which took place during one of Alex's good moods, but what benefits come from reflecting on the past? After all, hadn't their wedding lifted everyone's spirits at such a dark time? With the world at war, a wedding and a baby seemed an answer to their lives. And she, herself, has never forgotten the wonderful passion that existed between them during those days.

By the time John wakes her, she's snatched three hours of sleep. He sets a tray on her lap, pulls a chair up to the bed, and sits.

"Income tax is due soon," he says as they sip coffee and eat canned apricots and toast. "I need to see our accountant and move money around at the bank."

"I'll get something for dinner later, but first I'm setting our calendar for the cottage."

"Cass and Sam have never been for Victoria Day weekend. Sam would love it, and they'd be a help to open the cottage. They'd come if Adrienne would."

"I won't call Adrienne."

"I'll call them both. Next week, I'll take Adrienne to lunch. I need to talk to her about something else."

She's certain it's about the business he wants them to start. He finishes his toast, gets dressed in an elegant Italian suit, and kisses her goodbye. All she hears is him closing the door. While resting her head against the no-longer-plumped pillows, she stares out their window at the late-April sky. She could call Cass and tell her she's home, but the subject of Adrienne is guaranteed to surface. Besides, Cass will phone tomorrow, as always, when they're on their way out to go shopping.

After fetching her pocket calendar from her purse, she settles back to make summer plans. A list of cottage guests is at the back of her daybook. She turns the page and adds a few more names, then stops. She needs John's help to pick dates. Hopefully, they'll be communicating well enough to do that soon.

Suspecting she needs summer clothes, she goes through her closet and tosses unwanted items onto the bed. There's the ecru outfit she wore to her wedding with John, which she's kept, hoping to wear it again because of its cost. The secular service, performed by a justice-of-the-peace, took place at what was then his cabin and is now their cottage at Oxtongue Lake. Her daughters made potato, bean, and lettuce salads, corn-on-the-cob, and homemade ice cream. Graham grilled steaks, and they ate the wedding dinner under a tarpaulin, seated in lawn chairs the guests had brought themselves.

Conversely, her wedding to Alex was, for wartime, large and elaborate. Yet Alex's parents complained about the church in Ingersoll, the outdoor reception at Hillview Farm, the place settings of family china and silver, and the food of roast turkey, mashed potatoes, vegetables, cake, and ice cream. Only a few of the guests were members of London society. Instead, they were related to, had gone to school or church, played golf, or worked on the farm with Alex or her, so Hanna Muir treated them coldly.

Alex's grandparents helped plan the details and hosted it. Other than the honeymoon they spent on the train to boot camp, and the few steamy stretches they enjoyed during his positive periods, that wedding did nothing to enhance their married life. In contrast, her marriage to John has been more content. Still, keeping the ecru wedding dress in the hope she'll wear it again will have no effect on the state of their union now. He dislikes her rift with Adrienne, and despite his good nature, he'll soon retreat into one-syllable words. As Gloria wants to grow old with him, she needs to ask her friend Doris for some marital advice.

Still in her nightgown, she carries the breakfast tray to the kitchen and picks up the wall phone. When Doris answers, Gloria suggests lunch.

"Not today. I have to find receipts for income tax. Let's go one day next week."

"I need to talk now."

"What's the trouble?" Doris asks, her voice hesitant.

"Adrienne's miffed at me, and John's taken her side."

"Why are you surprised? He loves your girls. If he thinks Adrienne's right, he'll agree with her. Besides, Adrienne and Sam flew to Florida to see you, and you said John and Sam were inseparable. Why would you want to keep them apart?"

"My daughters are adults. I taught them to be polite. You know, if you don't have something nice to say, don't say anything. Don't ask personal questions. Let sleeping dogs lie. That sort of thing."

"Those rules went out with the sixties. If that's what you're looking for, I'm the wrong person to ask. I didn't let sleeping dogs lie. And what I said to Raymond wasn't very polite."

"Would you take it back if you could?"

"No. Not that our sex life has changed much, considering our age," Doris says, lowering her voice, "but Raymond is learning to touch me, and if you were honest with Adrienne, you might feel better."

"I can't do that," Gloria says, her voice breaking.

"What is it?"

"This reminiscing about Adrienne's father stirs memories I'd rather not discuss."

"Letting them fester gets between you and your girls, and Alex is dead, so what you say won't matter to him."

"Remembering him hurts, so talking would hurt more. Especially with his daughters."

"But in the end, you'd probably feel relieved. So would Adrienne and John. I wish I'd spoken to Raymond sooner. He was uncomfortable at first, but any move toward closeness is an improvement."

Gloria sucks in her breath, an image from the past clouding her mind. During Alex's dark periods of heavy drinking, intimacy between them was nonexistent. He'd fall asleep in his den night after night and go for days without washing. She'd cover for him with his bosses at the hospital, saying he was working at home. Meanwhile, she'd sleep in her sewing room. It was a wonder, during those black-dog days, he didn't soil himself. He seemed to know to empty his bladder or bowels. When it came to baths, she could sometimes lead him to the tub after the girls were asleep, undress him and coax him into the water. Leaning over the tub, she'd frantically scrub him like she had her babies, before he climbed out. After she'd shampooed his hair, he'd stand up and shake himself like a dog, muttering about "damned lice." She's sure those words came from a war memory, but he'd never told her anything from that time.

Although her need for his caresses inside her thigh, against her spine, or on her breasts was palpable as she washed him, he never became aroused. With Doris's mention of intimacy, she feels again the longing she'd get for him to return to the living, read to the girls, kiss her at the door, and wave goodbye. And it always corresponded with him drinking less, even drying out. Then, when he'd gone back to work, he'd insist she return to their bedroom and wear a black-silk nightgown with a plunging neckline he'd bought in Paris during the war. It was probably for Velma Miles, whose name he'd sometimes whisper during lovemaking. The nightdress had the slightest scent of *White Shoulders* perfume, maybe from Velma. But Gloria would stay silent, so needy was she for his touch. Though he seemed focussed on the mechanics of sex rather than its intimacy, he expected her, no matter how long he'd sat in the dark, to comply. In many ways, it was like Doris had described Raymond's lovemaking.

"Are you alright?" Doris asks.

"Lack of intimacy was a problem in my first marriage."

"Did you get help?"

"In the fifties, women were so glad to have their husbands home from the war, they put up and shut up. Then, as you know, he died." Gloria feels her cheeks dampen. "Yet Adrienne wants to talk about him."

"Obviously, it's painful. But your daughter has the right to ask. Now, I should go. Call me soon to tell me how you're doing."

"Okay," Gloria says and hangs up. She crawls under the covers, pulling the duvet over her head, and falls asleep.

When Cass doesn't phone before they go marketing on Saturday, John asks if she's not speaking to either daughter.

"She's probably at the university."

"You could call Sam."

"Let's go get groceries."

Long silences begin to burden their togetherness. Every day the following week, Gloria is glad when John leaves for his office, a suite at Yonge and St. Clair where he tracks his real-estate holdings and calls his broker. Things freeze between them until Thursday, when he comes home early with a bouquet of tulips.

While handing her the flowers, he says, "I'm having lunch with Adrienne tomorrow. She and Cass want to talk to you. It's up to you to patch things up."

Saturday morning, she dresses and is about to go to the soup kitchen when the phone rings.

"Can you find a cake recipe without eggs or milk?" her sister-in-law, Lucie, asks. "All we have for dessert is canned applesauce."

Three years ago, John had started a soup kitchen because he'd encountered a man outside the St. Clair subway entrance wrapped in a blanket and begging for money. The man reminded John of all the hungry people he'd known in the 1930s. As he wanted to do something, he asked the minister of a nearby church whether, with donations, they could use the hall to feed the hungry. When the pastor agreed, John involved everyone he knew to start the kitchen. And for his sister, Lucie, a retired dietitian, providing delicious, healthy meals for the needy became a second career.

While showering, Gloria remembers a recipe booklet her mother had used during wartime rationing. Neither eggs nor milk were rationed, but she recalled that this brochure had recipes for delicious food made with few ingredients, and she knows there's a cake in it that will do the job. She finds the pamphlet in a well-used manila envelope in the kitchen and dumps the contents onto the kitchen counter. The eggless, milkless recipe, sweetened with raisins, which was usually baked in a loaf pan, is there. Certain it would bake, multiplied, in sheet-cake pans, and knowing there are bags of raisins in the kitchen's pantry, she slips the booklet into her purse.

When she gets to the church, Gloria points out the recipe to Lucie and says, "If it works as a sheet cake, we'll serve it warm with applesauce."

"Sounds yummy," Lucie says. "Now, multiply the ingredients by four to mix it, then make that four times. Eight of our biggest pans should be enough to feed everyone."

As mixing four cakes and baking them, then making four more, is a big job, Gloria immediately turns on the oven to heat and begins measuring brown sugar into a pot. She heats it with water, adds shortening and spices, then stirs the syrup. A bouquet of nutmeg and cinnamon rises out of the pan and takes her back to the summer kitchen at Hillview, when she and Alex were courting. She'd made a spice cake with these flavours and iced it with Grandma Muir's coconut topping. As she knows there's unsweetened coconut in the pantry, too, she'll do the same with these.

After greasing the pans, she stirs in the rising agent, then spreads the batter into the tins. When the ring sounds to say the oven is heated, she puts four cakes into the oven and starts again. As she's stirring the next batch of syrup, she remembers how the Muirs never used milk. They had cream. This brings Alex to mind and how their whole lives were ahead of them when she'd learned to make this topping. Only years later, when he'd returned from war and she'd observed his catatonic behaviour in the den, did she understand what operating on those battle casualties had done to him. And until Adrienne started asking questions, that summer had faded with the decades.

She knows if she doesn't walk out of the kitchen now, she'll be in tears, weeping for Alex and his lost soul. The privileged life she lives now and the peaceful one she lived while he was at war have made it difficult for her to comprehend the horrors of battle. And now, as she works at the soup kitchen, she knows on some level it's a way to atone for how she didn't stop Alex's death.

Repeatedly, she's asked herself if she did everything she could to save him from the fractured existence he led on his return. Could she have stopped him from drinking? She always cooked his favourite foods so he didn't have room for another scotch, yet he rarely ate much. Although he himself was one, could she have found him a psychiatrist? Would that doctor have known how to treat him? She certainly could have replaced the lock on that gun box and hidden the key.

Through eyes blurred with tears, she sees John carrying a milk crate of boxed eggs across the church hall. He lifts his eyebrows at her from across the room. At that distance, she doubts he can see her sadness. As he gets close to the kitchen, she nods at him with as much dignity as she can muster. Then, without speaking to him, she slips through the back hall to the bathroom and locks herself in.

From outside, Lucie says, "Those last cakes need to go in." Gloria blows her nose and opens the door.

"Here's your purse," she whispers, handing it to Gloria. Without asking what's wrong, she adds, "Fix your makeup." Then she closes the door.

Gloria finds a makeup wipe in her bag, cleans her face, and reapplies foundation. If John's still here, he'll know she's been crying, but, like Lucie, he'll have the sense to keep quiet. She slips across the hall to the kitchen and finds him, sitting at the table near the window. After she removes the baked cakes from the oven, she puts in the last two. Then, she sits down next to him.

"Adrienne and I had lunch in a Vietnamese restaurant," he says. "The cottage is on for May. Cass and Sam will probably come too. That is, if you tell Adrienne everything she wants to know."

She turns to face him, wondering where she'll find the courage to talk about their father to her daughters and still keep the secret. Although she believes that her marriage, indeed her life, depends on what she says, she finds the strength to whisper, "I'll try."

December 23, 1943

Mud, blood, pain, death around me — have not slept in weeks. In R.A.P. on Ortona's outskirts — Jerries still hold north-west side — #3 C.I.B. taking return fire on north road into Ortona — stretcher bearers bring bodies as shelling continues — almost out of supplies — worry men sent for bandages won't return.

Last time jeep got through, some Christmas supplies arrived — Vino, Christmas pudding, but Vino and morphine don't mix — hate to deny anyone, including myself, such pleasures.

After Seaforths and 2nd Brigade took San Leonardo, got mired in ravine — mud made them targets for Jerries — most casualties fatal as stretcher bearers couldn't navigate mud — reinforcements got tracks moving again.

Seaforths, Royal Edmonton Regiment came against Jerries — 1st Parachute Division, 2nd Battalion trapped tanks by blocking side streets with rubble — our men went to surrounded main square — civilians, soldiers died, yet fighting continues — enemies meet face-to-face amidst centuries of stone, kill with bare hands — both sides blow up houses hiding enemies — soldiers suffocate, bleed to death under rubble.

Seen men, women crushed by tanks — we're now evacuating for battle fatigue and madness when men's souls left in mud with dead — am trapped here with no escape — want to get free, but can't — can't meet demands to save men — am exhausted — doubt I can go on.

Until Ortona, I thought that I could handle war — the dead will haunt me until I join them.

ELEVEN

Cass

Cass and Sam sit on the dock, their feet dangling in water. The air is brisk like a crisp apple, despite bright sunlight. A boat clips across the bay toward them, and Cass nods at the white sails, taut in the wind.

"Looks chilly. Maybe it'll warm up so we can go sailing tomorrow," Cass says.

"I don't care if it's cold. I love sailing with Grandpa," Sam says. "Did you spend your summers here when you were little?" She pulls her visibly shivering feet onto a towel.

"This was John's cabin. The first time I came here was for his wedding to Grandma Gloria. And once, before you were born, I came with your dad. He's always been an outdoor kind of guy."

"So you tell me," Sam says, drying each toe then pulling on her socks.

Cass finds it difficult to remember the details of her summers when she was little. Her mother would sometimes send her and Adrienne to day camp in one of Toronto's parks, the coolest place without air conditioning. Her one summer memory of her father, and it's only come since she and Adrienne have been discussing his death, was of him taking her fishing at a rented cottage. They were drifting in a small boat, their poles dangling in the water, when she felt a tug on her line. Her father moved to sit next to her, putting his hand above hers on the pole.

It wasn't hard to land the fish with her side resting against him as they pulled it in. She'd get the same secure feeling when she'd fall asleep on his lap, which she loved, while he sat in the den. After they reeled in the fish, he caught a bigger fish, and they proudly took them to her mother to clean.

"I thought we'd have to have tomato soup for dinner," her mother had said, hugging Cass. "Instead, my daughter is a fisherman."

"She even put the minnow on the hook," her father said as Cass basked in his pride.

"That's why I won't go fishing," Adrienne said. She'd come into the kitchen to be part of the excitement.

"Holding the minnow was yucky. And I don't like eating fish, but it was fun."

"We'll have fried potatoes, too," her mother said. "How's that?"

"Only if I can swim in my new bathing suit before we eat."

Her father laughed loudly and said if his new job went well, he'd buy a cottage. He kept laughing, and it lasted a long time. Finally, her mother said, "That's enough, Alex," and he stopped.

Cass looks across the water where breakers fleck the lake. Wind rustles white-pine needles and washes waves against the dock. She hears tires crunch on gravel and says, "Someone's here." It's Adrienne, and Cass is thankful she's arrived before their mother. That way, the sisters can plan what they'll ask her about their father's death.

After hugs and kisses, Adrienne opens her trunk and suggests Sam put the suitcase in the second bedroom on the right. Cass carries the cooler — a green, metal box she remembers from their childhood.

"You must have sold your car," Adrienne says, walking toward the cottage. She points to the Honda Civic parked next to her car.

"I got a good price for it, so I bought this little gem," Cass says, putting the cooler on the front porch. "A retired woman who only drove it to the grocery store owned it. It's got 25,000 km."

"Our old car was cool," Sam says.

"This car is functional, which is better than cool when saving money."

"Your payments must be lower," Adrienne says as she carries a carton of pop up the steps.

"Much. And I'll own the car sooner."

"Until we move to Vancouver and live with Dad," Sam says. "Then you won't need a car."

Adrienne raises her eyebrows as she deposits the carton on top of the cooler. Cass, who's told her sister about Eric's move back to Canada, puts her index finger to her lips, signalling silence. She doesn't want to encourage questions from Sam about Eric yet.

They find the key behind the front porch lattice work, where John told Adrienne it would be, and enter a large room. It faces both the lake and the road and serves as the kitchen and living room. Light filters through a crack in the plywood-covered window, making a shaft of dust.

"We should uncover the windows first," Adrienne says.

"That's not hard," Cass says. "They're attached with wing-nuts."

They store the plywood that covers the windows in the shed. With Cass consulting, Adrienne primes the pump and opens the water line to the lake. Cass plugs in the fridge, starts the hot water heater, and begins to dust. Sam vacuums the mattresses, then makes the beds with sheets from the cedar closet. She then vacuums the whole cottage and collapses on the couch.

"Why are they so late?" Cass asks. She has a damp cloth in her hand, and the scent of vinegar cuts the air.

"He called yesterday, when you weren't home, and said they'd be following his sailboat," Sam says, her face sheepish. "I forgot to tell you."

"A driver is pulling the boat from Florida," Adrienne says to Cass. "John says he's saving money by not storing it in Toronto over the winter then hauling it south every year. But it can't be that much. He should just rent a boat down there. He keeps telling me he wants to invest in my business."

"What business?" Cass and Sam ask together.

"That's the point. I just have a few clients who come to my house."

They laugh and go back to work. Sam takes the dishes out of the cupboard and washes the shelves. Then, she fills the sink with soap suds and starts on the glasses. Cass rubs each window with the vinegar-soaked cloth until it squeaks. Adrienne unloads the cooler's contents into the fridge, then grabs a tea towel and starts to dry.

"If I didn't know Grandma Gloria works at a soup kitchen," Sam says, stacking glasses in the drainer, "I wouldn't believe she washes dishes."

"True! She wants John to renovate and get a dishwasher here," Adrienne says. "He won't. He likes it rustic."

"He'd change his mind if Mom made him dry. When we were kids, Aunt Adrienne washed and I dried."

"And we'd fight. Once, Dad, I mean our real dad, came storming into the kitchen and said if we didn't stop, he wouldn't take us to the museum on Saturday. That shut us up."

Adrienne pauses, then says, "We must have been pretty young then. Later, when he drank all day, he couldn't take us anywhere."

The phone rings, and, having finished cleaning the windows, Cass answers it and relays the message.

"That was John. The guy with the boat was delayed at customs and just showed up. They don't want to launch the boat in the dark, so he's getting the driver a hotel room, and they'll drive up early in the morning."

"Lucky you brought food, Aunt Adrienne. Otherwise, we'd be hungry."

After dinner, Adrienne sets up a game of Monopoly on the dining table. As some of the old game's pieces are missing, they choose used buttons from Gloria's "at the cottage" jar to act as player pieces. Cass finds a woven one like those found on tweed jackets; Adrienne's is a black-jet bead like the ones on satin or brocade, and Sam finds a green frog from some discarded overalls. They play until Sam wins and goes to bed.

Adrienne puts away the board, and Cass asks, "Shall we usher in the weekend with some wine? My banker has allowed the odd bottle in my budget, bless her heart."

"I can't believe you're offering me a drink. I've virtually stopped. What did you bring?"

"A dry Australian red."

"I'll have one glass."

Cass finds some plastic glasses under the sink and puts them and the wine on the blanket-box coffee table.

"Let it breathe," she says and settles into a wicker armchair facing Adrienne. "So, what did you find on your trip to London?"

"Nothing much. While I was in the middle of dialing Aunt Margaret to find out when I should visit, Tony interrupted me, so I never talked to her. Without thinking to call again, I went anyway. But she wasn't there."

"So what did you do?"

"First, I took a cab to the address of our father's family home. It was a large, red brick two story that was probably considered grandiose when he lived there over fifty years ago. Its red brick made it stand out from the yellow brick of the surrounding homes, which were of the same vintage."

"Did you have the nerve to knock on the door?" asked Cass.

"I actually took a deep breath and asked the driver to wait while I did just that. When a young woman holding a baby answered, I asked her if her name was Muir."

"Wow. That was brave," says Cass. "She might have accused you of invading her privacy."

"She almost did. She looked straight at me with chilly eyes and said, 'There's no one here by that name.' Then she stepped back and closed the door, forcefully. There was nothing else for me to do but get back in the cab."

"It seems like you went to a lot of bother for that reaction."

"Of course I was miffed by her coldness, but then I decided I was glad to have at least found it. After all, I had no right to expect anything else. But seeing the house where he grew up made me feel closer to him, so I asked the driver to find where the china and hardware stores his parents had owned were."

"And?" asked Cass, sounding almost impatient.

"Well," and Adrienne pauses, which makes Cass want to shout at her in frustration. "The hardware store is a pub now. The china store, which isn't in the family anymore but still sells china, is called Muir's, which gave me a chill."

"Considering that I've kept the Muir name," Cass says, scratching her cheek, "it does me too."

"There's more to tell, but this might be too boring," Adrienne says and raises her eyebrows to Cass for a reaction.

"Not at all. As a sociology professor, even if I hadn't been fascinated and saddened by the letters you shared with me, I'm also concerned with the community that surrounded him as he was growing up."

After the wine has sat long enough, she pours them each a glass and hands one to Adrienne, nodding to her to finish the story.

"Well, after the cab driver let me out at the library, I found a family history by Margaret Muir and borrowed it to read in my hotel room. It contained a copy of Alex Muir's baptismal record. The next morning, I walked and found the church: Anglican and built of red brick like his family's home. It still towers, muted to pink, over the elegant but faded houses nearby."

"The area where he spent his childhood sounds like a well-heeled community," says Cass. "And the fact he grew up in that environment may have given him the strength to withstand what he experienced in the war. On the other hand, the mere contrast of his background compared to being a doctor in the war could cause trauma to his psyche."

"Can I finish my story?" asks Adrienne.

"Sorry. I thought you were."

"On my way home, I drove through Ingersoll and looked for Grandpa Muir's farm, but I realized, after driving around and reading the names on mailboxes, I needed precise directions. Aunt Margaret can tell us the exact location at the Muir reunion she's having on Canada Day. We're all invited."

"So you haven't asked her how Daddy died," Cass says, her

chair squeaking as she shifts position.

"I wanted to ask her in person, but she was away. I did get copies of his birth, marriage, and death certificates in the mail the other day."

"The death certificate might say."

"There's no place on it for the cause of death. And only certain people can request that information."

"I'm sure Mother could, but according to her, he had a heart attack."

"And I'm going to ask her again, for clarity. It's probably going to be painful, so I'm glad you're here to help."

Cass has nearly finished the bottle of wine. When she suggests Adrienne help empty it, her sister says, "Tony doesn't drink, and I'm giving it up ... for him."

"Big decision! And I've made mine about Eric."

"What's that?"

"He's in Vancouver looking for a house. This summer, we're going to visit him. If things go well, I'll look for a job there, or he could get one here. Whatever happens, we've decided to give us a chance."

"Who's decided?"

"Both of us. We talked for about an hour on Thursday night, and on our way up here, Sam agreed. He should have had this chance years ago."

"Or he should have given it to you," Adrienne says, and, in a gesture rarely used between them, hugs Cass as they pass in the hall on their way to bed.

The next morning, at the sound of a diesel engine, Cass looks through lace curtains hung years ago for her mother's wedding and sees a truck backing John's boat across the lawn.

Her bedroom door creaks open and Sam, dressed in shorts and a t-shirt, says, "They're here."

Her mother, wearing sunglasses and a wide-brimmed hat, sits in the front seat of John's car. She stares toward the boat launch while John stands behind the truck giving directions.

"Why don't you go out and ask her to come in?"

"Okay. Then I'm going to make French toast."

With Sam outside chatting, Cass washes, dresses in the clothes she wore yesterday, and goes to the kitchen where Adrienne leans against the counter, staring out the window.

"I almost wish Aunt Margaret hadn't sent those letters," Adrienne says, watching Sam help her grandmother out of the car. "I'm not sure I can . . . "

Sam opens the door and says, "Grandma wants some French toast." She pulls a chair out at the already set table for her grandmother to sit. "And Grandpa wants some too."

"We have to ask the truck driver to join us," Adrienne says.

"I already did, but he said no thanks. He has to leave as soon as the boat's off the trailer to keep his schedule."

Cass and Adrienne stand mutely at the sink while their mother hangs her jacket by the door. Stepping forward, Cass gives Gloria a kiss on the cheek, knocking her hat to the floor.

"It's good to see you Mom," she says. "The last time was Thanksgiving."

Adrienne retrieves the hat, hooking it over the jacket, and turns to say, "You look great." Their mother nods and sits at the table.

Sam, who's at the counter assembling ingredients, says, "I guess I'll make lots."

"Our trunk is crammed with food," John says. "After we eat breakfast, you girls can help your mother unload while Sam and I start rigging."

Sam has perfected her French toast recipe and brought butter, maple syrup, and mixed berries to complement it. Everyone but Gloria eats heartily, her usual approach to food.

While they're relaxing around the table before starting to clear, Adrienne says, "You're an excellent cook, Sam. You could go to Paris . . . study at Le Cordon Bleu. After all, you already know how to make French toast."

"That's an idea for sure, but what I really want to study is archaeology."

That's great," John says, "but we need to get busy and do our morning chores."

John and Sam go out and start rigging the boat while Adrienne and Cass bring in and put away all the food from John's car. It's enough for months, much of it non-perishable. Finally, Cass sits in the chair opposite Gloria, and Adrienne sits next to their mother in the living room area of the cottage.

"When he comes in, John will want to hear that we've finished this business about your father," begins Gloria.

"Let's get started then," Adrienne says.

"I've long ago put my life with your father aside, but I promised John I'd have this conversation. After your father died, I wanted to go back to teaching. My parents agreed, but the Muirs wouldn't hear of it."

"Why did they have anything to say about it?" Cass asks.

"The Muirs only cared about appearances. In those days, in wealthier circles, if a woman worked, even after her husband died, he was remembered for not providing," Gloria says, her expression lifeless.

"This is all very interesting," Adrienne says. "But we want to know how he died."

Turning to stare at her, Gloria says, "I've told you. He had a heart attack."

"We don't believe that. In the letters Aunt Margaret sent, there was one in pencil from 1959," Adrienne says. "I showed you this before." She pulls the paper from her pocket, placing it on the coffee table. "Aunt Margaret thought he wrote it while he was in hospital, but we don't remember him being sick."

Gloria rubs her hands up and down her arms anxiously, finally saying, "Well, he was. His drinking would get so bad, he'd black out. Then, he'd go to the hospital to dry out. When he was better, he'd go back to work with energy to burn. That is, until he was finally fired."

"What happened?" Cass asks.

"Originally, the doctors called it battle fatigue," Gloria says, her cheeks damp. "Although he never fought in the war, he cared for horribly injured soldiers. He'd be depressed, like he'd lost faith in the living, in doing anything. These times would happen when he'd been drinking heavily. Then, after he'd stopped . . . dried out, really . . . he'd cheer up and I couldn't slow him down."

"I've always thought of those as happy times," says Adrienne. "Like when he'd take us to the movies, buy us candy and popcorn, and let us watch the picture twice so we were really late getting home. You'd be furious with him, Mom."

"Maybe manic-depression," Cass says. "It's called bi-polar disorder now, and battle fatigue is called post-traumatic stress disorder . . . from the war."

"I know you're trying to help, Cass, but I think you should stop trying to diagnose him. You're a sociologist, not a psychologist," says Adrienne. "And giving his illness a fancy name doesn't make his drinking more acceptable. I think heavy alcohol consumption caused his moods, or, worse still, for him to black out, and I can say that with experience."

She nods at Cass and her mother as if to say, "I know about alcohol." Then, she gets a box of tissues from the kitchen, hands everyone a few, and says, "In his letters, the war sounds horrible."

"When he returned, he wasn't the same man," says Gloria. "He'd wake in the night, sobbing, and cry out about blood and severed limbs. He'd mention a woman's name. I think he drank to forget."

"Of course he did," Adrienne says. "But drinking causes depression, especially heavy drinking, and we think that killed him, or really . . . suicide did."

Gloria gasps and hides her face in her hands, her body racked with violent sobs.

Cass paces back and forth from her chair to the kitchen counter. On her second trip back, she stops and says, "I'm sure I heard the gun that day. Probably from hearing it before on the day Daddy shot at me."

"That never happened," says her mother, between sobs.

Cass has been staring at the ceiling while she talks. "We both know it did. I'm remembering more, right now, from the day he died. After the shot, you ran to see what had happened, Mother, and I followed. As you opened the door, I peeked around you from behind. Daddy was lying on the floor with something red growing next to him. I didn't know it was blood then, but I do now."

"Why don't you believe me?" Gloria says.

"Because I've finally remembered. You made a loud sound and sent me to my room. Then I heard other people in the house, probably the ambulance men. You came and got me. You said Daddy had gone to the hospital."

Through intermittent gasps for air, Gloria says, "That's impossible. I've told you. He had a heart attack. You have to stop saying suicide. There's no doubt his heart was broken. During the war, he loved Velma . . . wanted to be with her. It all happened so long ago."

"Oh no!" Adrienne says, her voice quivering. "I didn't know that, Mother. Your heart was broken, too."

She stands up from her chair and crosses to the couch, reaching to hug her mother, who's so busy wiping her tears that she doesn't lift her arms, and continues talking.

"When I figured out who she was, whose name he was calling in his sleep, my heart felt ripped from my chest. I'd loved him from the day I met him at university. Chemistry class, it was. I tried everything to make him happy, to get him to stop drinking."

"Like what?" Cass asks, trying not to sound accusing.

"Cooked food he liked, so he'd eat and not drink; took him for walks, so he wouldn't just sit; invited his war buddies, so they'd talk through their memories; I even tried to get him to go to A.A. Nothing worked."

"I can't believe he told you about the woman," Cass says.

"I figured it out. When he felt amorous, he made me wear a nightgown he'd brought back from France after the war," Gloria mumbles, staring at the ground. "It had a slight scent of *White Shoulders* perfume that I'd never worn. I deduced it belonged to Velma Miles because he called her name in his sleep"

"What a betrayal," Adrienne says. "But I do believe he loved you, too, Mother. I remember you dancing . . ." She pauses, and when her mother is finally calm, she continues. "Even though we think he shot himself, like he was probably trying to do when he missed shooting Cass, I need you to explain some things."

"Such as?"

"I wrote to the Surrogate Court and got a copy of his will. There was no life insurance mentioned. You always said, because of his insurance, you didn't have to work."

"Your father was terrible with money," Gloria says, beginning to weep again. "He'd let our insurance lapse before he had the heart attack."

"Killed himself, you mean," Adrienne says, "but what did you do?"

"I really wanted to go back to work." Seconds pass.

"But you didn't. So how did you raise us?"

"The Muirs set up a trust fund, and we lived on the interest." Gloria has wiped her eyes, and her voice is calmer.

"It must have been big, or interest rates were higher than they are now," Cass says.

"We managed."

"There's one more thing," Adrienne says. "I remember a box with a key in its lock that had a red ribbon dangling from it. Is that where he kept his gun?"

"I don't want . . . can hardly bear . . ."

"That must be yes! You say you did everything. Why didn't you take that key and hide it?" Adrienne says, trying not to sound critical.

Gloria is sobbing again. Cass stares at Adrienne and shakes her head back and forth, thinking they've pushed her far enough. Then Gloria begins to whisper, gasping for air between short bursts of speech.

"I knew I should. The next time he passed out from drinking, I looked everywhere. The key was gone. He must have hidden it."

Cass is silent, and Adrienne is white with shock.

After a long time, their mother says, "I think we've talked enough about this. We have to agree on what to say about how he died before John and Sam come back. If I can say he had a heart attack, you can say whatever you want. Just don't say it to me or John."

Cass and Adrienne stare blankly at each other. Then, Adrienne says, "I know he shot himself, and Cass remembers him dead on the den's floor, but if you admit he shot himself now but never again, this arrangement may work."

"Fine," says Gloria, and she leaves the room.

Later, Cass says, "Even though Mom saw the blood and the bullet wound, she just can't bear that he killed himself. It was the same for Dad. He couldn't bear his memories of the war. And later, when he became a psychiatrist, he hated himself more every day for getting fired because he couldn't help those battle fatigue victims."

"And, if this agreement is her way of telling the truth," Adrienne says, "I'll take it. Now, if we ever hope to have peace and be happy as a family, again, we need to stop hounding her about this."

After dinner, which Sam and John cook but no one else eats, Cass gets up, dries her eyes, and slips out the front door. She can hear Sam and John at the dock, using the last daylight to ready the boat. Cass is grateful for their friendship and sad, even now, that it's not her father teaching Sam to sail. She always loved him — loved sitting on his lap, loved listening to the interesting things he said when he still talked, loved everything about him, as only an innocent child can. And now, because of what he suffered, which no one should ever have to experience, she can accept and even be comforted knowing that he killed himself to stop the torment.

She hikes along the road leading to the highway and kicks stones at nearby trees. Here and there along the shoulder, fiddleheads unfurl. She knows these plants are edible. Tomorrow, she could collect some for dinner. Hearing a tree frog's trill, she sits on a roadside bolder as the woods darken. A clutch of trillium gleams like stars in the nearby underbrush. Later, she climbs off the rock and turns back to the cottage. A bulky form stumbles through the twilight toward her, and her neck bristles. A bear, a moose, or maybe the Sasquatch, she speculates — though she's not sure, despite legendary stories, that seeing any of these is common in Muskoka.

"The boat's ready," says a voice she recognizes as John's. "Adrienne says she'll come for a sail if you will."

"What about Mother?"

"I made her some tea and helped her to bed." His white Tilley hat is now reassuringly visible in the twilight.

John hurries down to the boat, where Sam and Adrienne wait. Cass goes inside to change. The refrigerator's hum startles her. In her room, she pulls on jogging pants and a sweatshirt, then pauses at her mother's door. A sound, like a mewing kitten caught in a cardboard box, is barely audible through the wood.

Electric lanterns in the trees next to the stairs light the way as she walks. Crossing the beach, she stumbles and catches herself, thinking of her mother. Cass wants to go back, fling open the bedroom door and say, "We could have helped him," but she knows her mother would say, as they've agreed, "How can you stop a heart attack?"

Sam and Adrienne sit in the boat, lifejackets fastened, as John helps Cass aboard. When they're far enough offshore, with the sails slack, he encourages Sam to help him tack.

Cass taps Adrienne on the knee and asks, "Are you alright?"

Adrienne turns her head and whispers, "Even though Mom has found a way to admit he did it without saying it, I know he killed himself. He was depressed from drinking. He felt hopeless that all he'd done to save his comrades wasn't enough. What I don't get though is why no one told us. People love gossip."

"In those days, people didn't talk about awful things," Cass says. "That way, it was thought they'd be forgotten. But, ironically, those memories are the ones that never leave us. After all, I heard the gun, and now I've remembered."

"Hearing it put you in shock, so you forgot," John, who's been eavesdropping, says. "Sometimes, after something terrifying happens, people block it out for emotional protection. You both know that."

Cass is thankful Sam is busy staring at the sky through binoculars.

If she's listening to this conversation, she's not acknowledging it. Instead, she says, "I want to learn about the stars."

John points to the right with one hand while the other holds the steering wheel. He helps Sam find the Little Dipper, then says, "See that bright star at the end of the handle?"

"Yes."

"That's Polaris. The North Star. No matter what month, it's always in the north. You can use it to figure your direction, and the Big Dipper moves in a circle around it."

They continue floating in the boat while John and Adrienne teach Sam about Arcturus and Ariadne's gem-laden crown, which Bacchus gave her when they married. John explains how, when she died, Bacchus placed the crown, Corona Borealis, in the heavens, and it appears there every spring.

"There it is," Sam says. "It sounds like Aurora Borealis. Any relation?"

They all laugh, and Adrienne says, "It's beautiful tonight," her voice echoing against the lake's surface. "We should celebrate your birthday here, Cass."

"Great idea," John says, "But you'll be living in Vancouver."

"I could ask Eric to come with us for the weekend."

"The renovations won't be finished, so there might not be room."

"You could all come to my house," Adrienne says. "Then, we could celebrate John's and Mom's here, at Thanksgiving. And you could meet Tony."

"Now you're talking," John says.

"Adrienne," Cass whispers. "Thanks for caring about those letters. I think reading them helped us understand Dad, brought us closer, and gave us some peace about his death."

"Will you play Monopoly with us when we get back, Grandpa John?" Sam asks, as if she wants to change the subject.

"As long as your grandmother doesn't need me," he says and turns the boat in a wide arc toward home.

February 19, 1944

At Caserta in psychiatric hospital where Dr. Doyle put me after I couldn't help anyone. Still trying to erase memories of men who've lost limbs, gone blind, deaf — who beg me to shoot them so won't suffer.

Many men come with offal spilled out, stinking, legs crushed by tanks — they thought I was God or miracle maker in foul-smelling heaven.

Missed Christmas dinner in Ortona. In the horror, someone set tables, cooked roast pork for the allied and German soldiers and they sat together — a Christmas miracle — if there, I would have proudly served soldiers from both sides, as other officers did.

Velma Miles here. Reads, sings, feeds me for strength — we play cards, walk, do things I won't write here — she listens to my guilt for maimed, dead men — understands what trying to heal broken bodies means — if I get home, won't tell anyone.

Nothing in med school prepared me for the dust and the heat and the mud-filled river valleys flowing with blood — nothing prepared me for the killing.

Near New Year's, Grant Chapman blown up by land mine — if I hadn't been evacuated, he would've been brought to me in pieces — his parts gathered on stretcher, delivered to R.A.P., identified by letter from mother he carried — thankful I didn't see his end — he was my friend throughout this bloodbath — I'll never forget him — if I'm still alive at Christmas, the sadness I'll feel remembering him then will be tribute to his goodness.

TWELVE

Adrienne

After she's called Aunt Margaret and arranged to visit her, Adrienne is pleased that she visited London earlier, while her aunt was away. Being alone meant she could explore the places important to her father, without feeling she was ignoring Margaret. Now that she's made plans, she sips coffee at the kitchen table and stares through the patio doors at a crab-apple tree teeming with pink blossoms. Its outrageous beauty makes her want to grab a camera and have the shot she takes framed. It's odd that after an emotional weekend with her mother, she can feel joy from such a sight. She knows, even if she'd missed piano lessons, her father would still have killed himself, and she accepts that as his right. He needed to ease his suffering. Of course, reading the letters Aunt Margaret sent made her want to know more about his death. And now that she knows the truth, and she and her mother have agreed to disagree, Adrienne wants to go forward with her life.

She's made appointments with Barb, Norm, Leon, and Lucy for tomorrow. Thursday, she'll meet John about his business idea and contact some additional potential clients Jessica has found. Sometime before Friday, when she hosts the Astronomy Club, she'll buy some drinks to go with the refreshments Dell is bringing to replace the ones she made for his meeting. Her calendar, now colour coded for research, personal, and client meetings, is more interesting than when she had a job.

She enters the security code, after shopping for the meeting and opens the door as the phone rings.

"I called earlier, but you were out," Tony says. "I bought some fresh tuna and asparagus. Come for dinner."

"Bring them here, and we'll throw them on the grill."

"I'll be there at six."

She lies down on the living room couch to finish the newspaper, and the next thing she hears is the doorbell. Tony is standing under his sensor lights. He kisses her on the lips and his tongue lingers. His hand creeps under her sweater as he caresses her breast through her clothes. In response, her body begins to tingle, and she feels him, hard against her.

"There'll be lots of time for this later," she says and kisses him. "But I'm hungry now, so let's get started on dinner."

After the barbeque is lit, he sets the table with utensils and says, "I know you're going to visit your aunt soon, but how long since you've seen her?"

"Last time was a few years after my father shot himself."

"You can say died. You don't have to tell everything. I don't tell people my first wife's dead."

"I didn't know you had a second," she says, turning to face him from her place at the sink. She feels anger rising in her that he's lied, or at least withheld this from her.

"Oops. Freudian slip. I've only ever had one wife." He leans over and kisses the base of her neck. "Just wishful thinking. Anyway, if it's been that long, why did you contact her?"

She takes deep breaths to quell her temper then finally smiles at his error.

"Sorry about that. I thought you'd lied to me. After my father died, we always sent cards and gifts. Then she sent me my father's letters. It follows that we'd meet. But now, I have nothing to say."

"I'll bet she doesn't know about his suicide. Everyone seems to have hidden the secret well," he says and puts salt and pepper shakers on the table.

"Cass and I made an agreement with our mother about how

we'd talk about his death. But I wonder if Margaret knows and she wanted me to know too."

"Agreement?" he asks.

"She'll say a heart attack killed him, and we'll say whatever we want, except to her or John."

"You could still ask Margaret. Or maybe, more importantly for you, let the pain go. Concentrate on other things, like meeting my boys."

"They're hardly boys. But yes, I'd like to meet them. Right now, though, I'm hungry, so can you please check the fish?"

Tony goes out, shutting the patio door behind him. She watches him open the barbecue lid, handsome in jeans and a golf shirt. Smoke rises and fills the air with a salty smell. Behind where he stands on the deck are the last of the tulips, still blooming because of the deck's shade, a few pink petals painting the ground. She opens the glass patio door and holds out a clean platter.

"It's your business how you spend your time," he says, reaching for it, "but I sure hope some of it is with me. And don't be so obsessed with the past that you miss out on the future."

As her appointment with Barb is for nine, Adrienne gets up early to tidy the den. Since their last meeting, she's registered herself as *Adrienne Adams Financial Services* and sent out an announcement to potential clients. She's seen her lawyer, created letterhead and all the forms she'll need to do business. She serves coffee to Barb, then gets busy suggesting financial solutions to Josh's trust. They discuss the pros and cons of setting up a monthly payment to cover his expenses.

Finally, with the paperwork finished and signed, Barb says, "Even the parking here is better than downtown."

As soon as Barb leaves, Norman arrives. He's looking slightly healthier than the last time she saw him.

"I know what you're going to say," he says, before she can even say hello. "I know I'm getting better. I'd lost so much weight, I thought it was a cancerous tumour the doctors couldn't find.

Instead, it was worms I'd picked up from somewhere." Then his face brightens with a smile.

"With such good news," says Adrienne, "What could you possibly need today?"

Norman's face becomes serious again. "I live with my mother and support her financially. For a while, I thought I was going to die, so I need to make sure she's supported if I die first."

When Adrienne asks him to describe his assets, she's surprised to learn that he has a designated pension from the big chemical firm where he's employed. He also owns the home outright where he and his mother live. And he has investments.

"Norman. You're well off. Depending on how long you live, there'll be unspent pension funds you should leave to your mother as well as the house, which she could sell, then live off the profits. Leave her any additional investments you have as well. She'll be fine."

"That's a relief," he says. "But what if I marry someone and move out?"

"Sign this paperwork to transfer your investments to my care, but you'll have to talk to a lawyer about transferring the house to her," she says. "As for your marriage, you may need a psychologist to help you wade through the financial minefield that would create between the survivors."

Norman seems to want to stay around to talk, but when Leon arrives, he promptly shakes both their hands and leaves.

"How can I help you today, Leon?" starts Adrienne.

"My problem," says Leon, "is that my wife inherited a large amount of money. I mean really large."

When Adrienne's mouth drops at the amount, Leon says, "So you probably wonder why I'm talking to you at all."

As Adrienne nods, he says, "She spends so much money every day that I have to invest some to protect our old age."

"That shouldn't be a problem," says Adrienne, and she lays out some options for him. "But first, you have to get her to agree that it's important to secure your future together. Do that, then come back and see me. Better yet, bring her too."

"I'll try," says Leon, and he waves goodbye through her office window as he departs.

As soon as he starts his car, the phone rings and Cass says, "How are you?"

"I'm gradually getting better."

"Good. You have great things happening in your life, like falling in love with Tony, and we're friends now, too. In a strange way, those letters brought us back together."

"You're right. Now, how are your plans for visiting Eric?"

"Terrifying. I don't know whether I can live with another adult."

Adrienne sits down at the kitchen table and says, "I'm not one to give advice. My marriage failed miserably, and I didn't have a child to consider. All you can do is try."

"Look at Mom and how she stuck out Dad's depression and drinking," Cass says. "Now that's diligence. If she can do that, I should be able to make a go at this marriage."

"It's obvious she loved him. And now we've agreed to disagree. That's all good . . . right?"

"I hope so," says Cass.

They spend some time talking about how Sam is doing at the thought of visiting her father, then Adrienne mentions that her final client for the day should be arriving soon, and she needs to eat something before that.

"Okay," says Cass. "We'll talk soon," and she hangs up.

Adrienne immediately goes to the kitchen and eats the last night's leftover salad from the fridge. She's just finished brushing her teeth when the doorbell rings.

She ushers Lucy into the den and sits down at her desk. After they talk briefly about how Lucy has persuaded the school board to give her a higher grade to teach, Adrienne says, "But you have to keep teaching and work on your business at night and on the weekend, until it can support you."

When Lucy looks downhearted, Adrienne says, "Here's how you become a sole proprietor of a business," and she hands her a pamphlet. "You have to choose a name. Then you have to go to the bank and ask for a loan."

"I've saved quite a bit of money toward this already," says Lucy. "I thought I'd start small, selling my products to family and friends from the Chinese community."

"That's what I'd advise," says Adrienne. "Then, when it grows so big you need money to expand, you could seek investors rather than taking loans."

Lucy is laughing now, her laugh like a brook, babbling in a forest. "If this business gets that big, I'm sure I could find investors. Maybe even my parents, if they ever get over my quitting teaching."

"I might even be interested," says Adrienne, and she suddenly sees the irony of how she probably lost her job over an argument she'd had with her CEO about supporting a charity that helps people start businesses. Lucy wasn't unemployed or underemployed, but Adrienne was happy to help her, and she certainly deserved to start a business.

To the waiter, John says, "I'll have the macaroni and cheese." He's sitting with Adrienne near a window at Fran's, overlooking St. Clair West.

"And I'll have an egg salad on brown," Adrienne says.

He's walked over from his office to meet her and looks overheated in his suit and tie. For the end of May, it's unseasonably humid, and his hair curls uncontrollably. They sip ice water, and he finally says, "I think, because your mother seems happier, you and she have made peace."

"We've come to an agreement. Although she all but admitted he killed himself, she still wants to say he had a heart attack. And I'm not to tell you or her that he killed himself, but I can say what I think to anyone else. It still perplexes me, because I know she knows. Why can't she say it?"

"I believe that he killed himself, like you told me. Don't you think, after what the war did to him, it's understandable? I'm sure she did everything she could to help him, so she shouldn't feel guilty about his death. But I think she does, and that's why she can't say it."

John loosens his tie, undoes his top button, and continues. "Besides, he was an adult. She'd have to have locked him up to protect him from himself."

"I've come to terms with him killing himself. He must have been tortured by memories."

Although she thought she'd accepted his suicide, Adrienne hears her voice — thick, trembling, and close to tears.

"From what I know about post-traumatic stress disorder and the numbers of Vietnam veterans who've died by suicide, soldiers don't talk about the horror. They choose another way to deal with it."

The waiter refills their water glasses. He brings lunch, and they eat in silence. Adrienne nibbles on her sandwich, and John has several bites of macaroni before he speaks again.

"I have other things to talk to you about, but first I want to say one thing. Given the circumstances, your mother did her best with you girls. And although you both have issues, one about money and the other drinking, everyone I know has issues, and from what I can see, you're both managing to work through those."

"Thank you, John," she says and hesitates before continuing. "If it's not too personal, what I want to know is why you weren't so depressed after the war that you killed yourself? You were interned, and then you fought. My father didn't see the battlefield, only the results, and yet ..."

John clears his throat and says, "Until I met your mother, I only thought about myself. Is that depressed?"

"You didn't hurt yourself."

"It boils down to two things. Trauma and chemistry. Although I felt unjustly imprisoned, I only saw one minesweeper explode. Your father saw men every day who'd been blown to bits. And he was expected to save them, but often failed. As for body chemistry, only God and DNA have control over that."

"When I got those letters, I had no idea what effect reading and sharing them would have on our family," she says.

"You'll get past this. Years ago, right or wrong, your mother thought it best not to talk about him to you girls. And you've handled this suicide idea better now than you would have as children. Anyway, I'd rather talk about business. It's less disturbing." He finishes his macaroni and pushes his plate aside. "When you first lost your job, I thought I wanted to start a business with you. Now, I want to retire. I need someone to manage my properties. You could move into my office and look after my assets. I'd pay you, and you could meet clients there."

The waiter, who's clearing the table, says, "Would you like anything else?"

"Coffee for us both, please," John says. "And two orders of plum cake." Adrienne is about to object when he says, "You only ate half a sandwich."

He raises his eyebrows, waiting for her to speak. When she doesn't, he says that her mother wants Adrienne and Cass to have the money left from the trust fund the Muirs set up and from the sale of her house. Then, he asks Adrienne, again, if she'll look after his assets, and she says she'll consider it.

"You now know that he killed himself, but you and Cass suffered from his death, and with this money, Cass can put a down payment on a house."

"If she doesn't move to Vancouver."

"She has to live somewhere. And if she and Sam move, we'll certainly miss them. But we're still giving you girls the money. As for my business, I'll be doing renovations on the cottage all summer, so we can wait until fall."

"How did Mom finally persuade you to renovate?"

"We want to spend more time there. Sam likes it, and maybe she'll visit by herself. Or, if she moves to Vancouver, her visits will be fewer but longer."

After dessert, they sit drinking coffee and talking. Adrienne discovers that John is plugged in to the global marketplace. He trades stocks in Tokyo and New York via the internet, and he and Gloria plan to travel to Japan. Adrienne knows that managing his business wouldn't be boring.

By mid-afternoon, he puts a generous tip on the table, gets up, and says, "I'll walk you to your car. And, by the way, your mother and I are going to the reunion picnic. She's a bit nervous about it, but I think it's important."

"That's fantastic," Adrienne says. "No need to be nervous. It'll be fun."

Outside, the heat is so intense she sees waves radiating from the sidewalk. Away from the air conditioning, John looks more uncomfortable every minute.

She gives him a ride, and when she drops him at his office, he says, "Thanks for this talk, Adrienne," and waves as she pulls into traffic.

With the bottled water, juices, and pop in the fridge, ready for her meeting and half-an-hour to kill before it starts, Adrienne drags the electric broom to the third floor. She shoves it around, then wipes every surface with a damp cloth and calls the room clean. Her passion for the stars has waned lately, and though her meeting with John held very positive surprises, she's tired and wishes she'd cancelled the gathering.

When the whole group has arrived and she's helped Dell put the food he brought on trays, they move to the third floor, and Dell and Sonia begin a contest on who can find Vega or Scorpius first.

"There's Vega," Dell finally shouts. "I beat you, Sonia." She goes to stare through his binoculars. Everyone congregates near them to have a look. They've all made log entries, which are read aloud.

When it's Adrienne's turn, she hesitates, then says, "I haven't entered this, but I spent last weekend at Oxtongue Lake. We saw Arcturus and Corona Borealis."

"Muskoka's a great place to star gaze," Dell says. "Don't forget. The August meeting is at my cottage on Lake of Bays."

Adrienne says, "I know we'll see the heavens there."

Inside the retirement home's front door, a woman with chin-length white hair stands next to the fireplace. She glances at Adrienne then rushes forward.

"You must be Adrienne Muir," she says, looking like she's known Adrienne all her life.

"Aunt Margaret?" Adrienne asks and holds out her hand. "It's actually Adrienne Adams. Don't ask me why, but I kept my husband's name."

"And you stand exactly like your father did. Give me a hug, for old time's sake, and I'll show you my room. Then we'll have tea. It's such a thrill to see you."

Despite her slightly stooped appearance, Margaret is still taller than most women. Dressed in a tailored suit and white shirt with a starched collar, she leads Adrienne rapidly down a long hall. She stops at a door with a wallpaper border of books around its frame. Inside her small suite, every possible surface is covered with full bookshelves. A table under the window holds a desktop computer with piles of books all around it.

"Please, sit down," she says and motions for Adrienne to sit near the window. She sits opposite and asks, "Do you like my suite?"

"I can certainly tell you were a librarian with all these books. It's lovely."

"It's smaller than my Calgary penthouse, but it's home."

"Why did you move?"

"To be closer to family, before it's too late for me to enjoy them." Margaret pulls down her skirt to cover her knees. "Aunt Muriel, your dad's and my father's sister, had four daughters, and some of their children live near here."

At the mention of her father, Adrienne breathes in sharply and her mouth feels dry. She asks, as a way of diverting her aunt's attention, how close Margaret is to them.

"When I sold Hillview Farm to Muriel's granddaughter, Judy, we started to correspond. Sort of like you and I have."

"So that's what's become of the farm."

"If you come to the picnic, you'll see it. Anyway, I'll bet you want to talk about your father, but if we don't go to tea now, the best cakes will be gone."

Adrienne follows her out the door. As she's locking up, Margaret says, "I meant to show you one of my scrapbooks." She goes back and returns with a black album secured with a ribbon.

In the dining room, groups of grey-haired or bald people are clustered around tables of four. Antique wicker armchairs line the walls and spill out the sliding glass doors to the shaded portico. A garden, green with trees, lies beyond.

"I want to get a table in good light," Margaret says and leads Adrienne to a spot by the patio doors. They sit down opposite each other and a woman, dressed in a cream-linen pantsuit, stops at their table.

"This has to be a Muir," she says, looking curiously at Adrienne.

"Lilian Gordon, this is Adrienne Adams, my niece, one of Alex's daughters. Adrienne, this is my friend Lilian. She was in my class at university. She's a librarian, too."

"Margaret and I are old friends," Lilian says, reaching out to pat Margaret's hand. "And there was a time when I thought your father was the bee's knees." She smiles, her eyes full of mischief.

As Lilian moves along, Adrienne says to Margaret, "I'm surprised anyone in London still remembers my father."

"A lot of the old timers are dying off, but there are more than a few who knew the Muirs. Now, let's have a look at this book while we wait for our tea."

On the cover, in white lettering, is the title *Hillview Farm, 1924 – 1944*. The items are attached with old fashioned photo mounting corners for easy removal. Contained on the pages are mementos, joined together with Aunt Margaret's narrative, written in perfect script. Adrienne and Margaret ramble through the album, remarking on certain items.

One photo shows a young man sitting on an empty wagon, a pitchfork in his hand. He wears striped overalls and a long-sleeved shirt. His hair sticks out from under his straw hat.

July 1929. Alex haying. That summer, he worked harder than the hired help, and I learned to make pastry.

A *London Free Press* newspaper clipping, dated Wednesday, October 30, 1929, has the headline "STOCK MARKET CRASHES".
The crash didn't affect us, but the depression that came after it did. Luckily, the Muirs owned land and animals, so we had enough food, and our father, who owned two stores, was careful with his money. We got by.

In another photo, two girls wearing aprons, their hair tied in kerchiefs, sit on a swinging porch seat. A large black dog sleeps at their feet.
August 1932. Rose and I spent time together at Hillview. It was so hot that everyone but us took a nap. Even the men, who'd work long after sunset when it had cooled off, had to lie down in the fields mid-day.

A newspaper clipping from the *London Free Press*, this one dated September 3, 1939, has the headline "GREAT BRITAIN & FRANCE DECLARE WAR ON GERMANY".
This news came as no surprise. Then Canada declared war. Alex's medical program was accelerated so he could graduate and go overseas with the R.C.A.M.C.

The next item is a letter pasted into the scrapbook.

May 1943

Grandpa Muir,
The letter finally came that the baby was born dead and no one could do anything, and even though I wasn't there, the baby died anyway. Gloria didn't die, but she wouldn't talk, and she and her parents had a service at the hospital chapel. Mother and Father didn't go, probably because it wasn't at their church, or the minister wasn't Anglican, or services for dead babies aren't done. I'm sure if Mother had told you about the service, you and Grandma would have gone, but they weren't kind enough to support their daughter-in-law in her grief. How could any of this have happened?
A.

For a long time, neither of them says anything. Finally, Adrienne asks, "Why didn't you write under this?"

"There was nothing to say. The letter upset Grandpa terribly. Alex was his only grandson."

The dining room is almost empty. Dishes clink as kitchen staff clear then brush crumbs from the tables.

"The staff want to set up for dinner," Margaret says and closes the album.

Adrienne is pleased at how much she likes Margaret and how the pictures and narrative in this book make her feel like she's found family.

"The Rose in these pictures is Judy's mother, right? And Judy bought Hillview. Tell me the names of Rose's sisters again."

"Erin, Kathleen, Maeve, and Patricia. You'll get to meet all of them but Maeve at the reunion. She died of a heart attack last summer."

"I'm sorry to hear that. If I'd known, I would have gone to the funeral or sent a card."

Adrienne thinks of asking if heart problems run in the family, but stays quiet.

"You are coming, aren't you? We're hoping your sister, Cass, will come too. I guess it's too much to expect your mother."

"I saw John, her husband, the other day, and he says they're coming. And so am I. Cass and Sam will too. Thank you for the invitation."

After Margaret closes the scrapbook, she holds it in her left hand, and she and Adrienne get up and walk to the door of the retirement home.

"I'm so glad you took the time to come and visit me," Margaret says. "And I'll look forward to seeing you all at the reunion."

"Yes, we've come a long way to get to the point of agreeing to come, but it was worth it. Now, we can feel like we're part of a family."

As she enters the eastbound highway ramp, Adrienne turns on her lights. Lombardy poplars throw long, late-afternoon shadows over the fields. Fences blur against the newly sprouting ground. She whizzes past exits for towns and barely notices the Ingersoll sign. Sometime before the reunion, she'll ask Tony to help her find Great Grandpa Muir's farm. She recites the names of Muriel's daughters under her breath: Erin, Kathleen, Maeve, Rose, and Patricia. Some she'll meet at the Canada Day picnic. They are her long-lost family members who she hopes will be her friends, as Margaret is now.

The picnic will be the first Muir reunion in fifty years. According to Margaret, Dominion Day changed after the war. It sounds like everything did, including her father.

"Judy and I want to have fun and do the things we did at those picnics," Margaret had said.

Because she had to ask, Adrienne interrupted, saying, "Although our mother will tell you a heart attack killed him, I think she says that to preserve appearances. Cass and I know he shot himself, and so does she. Cass heard the gun and saw the blood. What's your opinion?"

Her chest feels like it's in a vice as she waits for the answer.

"My word," says Margaret, and she reaches for a tissue that's tucked into her suit's cuff. "This comes as a huge shock. I don't want to think that. He was my dearest friend. We only had each other." By now, she's dabbing at her eyes. "Mother and Father were always working, and they didn't have much time for us. Besides, they weren't affectionate. I can barely remember my mother hugging me."

"We didn't want to think that either," Adrienne says, "Nobody did," but Margaret has started talking again.

"By then, I was living in Calgary. I came home for the funeral, but I never saw his body. Neither my parents nor yours believed in open caskets, and I didn't want to ask to see him, in case it hurt them. Besides, it seemed too grizzly." Then, she added, "Your mother did tell me he'd had a heart attack, but suicide wouldn't surprise me. He was so changed by the war; it destroyed him."

Adrienne listened to Margaret explain how Oliver and Harriet Muir, who had lived in that very retirement home at the time of her father's death, gave their son, Gordon, money for Alex's family.

"And this was a secret. Right?"

"That's what it's like in this family," Margaret said. "What convinced you it was suicide?"

"Remember that note we found in the letters? From that, we figured it out."

Margaret put her arm around Adrienne and said, "We had such hopes for you girls. And I think they've come to pass. Oh, I just remembered. There's something on my shelf I want to give you. Come back to my room before you go?" At the book-filled space, Margaret hugged Adrienne and handed her something in a wrinkled, brown bag.

"I found it when I was looking for this," and she taps the album with her free hand. "I hope it's helpful."

Adrienne walked outside and got in her car, knowing her idea of ordinary and how she'd known, even as a child, that she did not want such a life, had changed. Recently, she'd learned that the most ordinary things can be extraordinary. She knew that discovering her father was driven to suicide by war, that her lover had battled alcohol to become a good father, and that her sister, niece, and stepfather had lived their lives while supporting her in finding answers about her own life were all ordinary things. And, even though Gloria still denied, publicly, how Adrienne's father had died, she knew the denial was based on love. Indeed, these most ordinary things were made extraordinary by love — another thing as ordinary as the stars. If these things and the extended family she'd discovered were ordinary, she'd gladly make them part of her life.

She slows the car to get her bearings and sees she's passed the Cambridge, Kitchener/Waterloo, and Guelph exits. She's making good time, but she won't be home by seven, the time she'd told Tony to expect her. Though it's still light, she sees, through the front windshield, the earliest star in the night sky. She stops the car on the right shoulder and gets out. Although she can't remember what's visible in this part of Ontario before twilight, she sees a luminous globe, low and languid, and knows it must be Venus, goddess of love. She smiles to herself, thinking how appropriate to see that star while she's driving home to Tony.

She gets back in the car, knowing he'll have picked up something, maybe fresh pasta and sauce, then let himself in and started dinner. When she gets there, he'll kiss her, and then he'll ask about Aunt Margaret. Adrienne thinks of how she's come to care for him and what knowing him and his life's story has added to her own. In particular, they've found an activity they both enjoy: travelling. And he's told her he'd like to do some hiking and camping with her. Things she, as a high-powered financial advisor, never considered. She thinks, too, of all the time she spent going to the library, reading her father's letters, and staring at the stars with her astronomy club friends. She should make that scrapbook and a copy for Cass. Such visible proof of this journey they've taken together will improve the bond that's growing between them.

A transport truck pulls up behind her, and she moves over to let him pass. She spots a billboard for a service centre at the next exit and pulls into the far-right lane. As she pulls off the highway, she sees cars are lined up at the drive-through, but she gets in behind the last vehicle and inches forward, car by car. While resting her head on the steering wheel, her eyes drift to the brown paper package on the seat. She reaches the drive-thru window and orders her coffee. After parking, she opens the package. Inside is a small, leather-bound book; on top is a note in her father's handwriting.

September 1959

Dear Margaret,

Here is the diary I wrote in the war. It says things I'd rather Gloria not see, like the time I spent in a psychiatric centre as a patient, then a doctor. Please keep it safe. I don't know when anyone will want to read it, but I'd rather forget.

A.

With her heart pushing against her breastbone, Adrienne decides to call Cass the minute she gets home and tell her about this find. She places the parcel back in the bag and keeps driving.

By the time she exits at Allen Road, cars fill all the lanes on the 401. She inches along and sees, to her right, her mother's favourite shopping centre, which makes Adrienne think of how Gloria's life includes John, something for which she'll be eternally thankful. Tears cloud her eyes, but now they're not because she's sad. They're because she's thankful. She turns onto her street and into her driveway, where she can wait no longer. Carefully, she lifts the leather-bound book from the bag, opens it, and begins to read.

October 15, 1938

Gloria gave me this diary to help me keep track of my life when I left her and her parents in London. She wants me to write things that happen while I'm studying medicine at the University of Toronto. Writing in a diary helps her understand her feelings, and she thinks it will also help me. She promises to never ask to read what I write, and I'll do the same for her.

Living here is a big change from living at home while I took my undergrad at Western . . .

From inside the car, she sees the kitchen light shining down the hallway and through the glass panels by the front door, and she knows Tony is making dinner.

GLOSSARY OF MILITARY ABBREVIATIONS

AC/AC barrage-	Aircraft Barrage
Arty. -	Artillery
A.D.S. -	Advanced Dressing Station
A.F.S. -	Ambulance Field Service
AWOL -	Away Without Leave
Batt'n -	Battalion
B.D.S. -	Beach Dressing Station
Cas. -	Casualty
C.C.S. -	Casualty Clearing Station or Critical Care Station
C.G.H. -	Canadian General Hospital
Coy. -	Company
D.O. -	Dental Officer
F.D.S. -	Field Dressing Station
F.S.U. -	Field Surgical Unit
1st Can. Div. -	First Canadian Division
M.D.S. -	Medical Dressing Station
M.O. -	Medical Officer
#1 C.I.B. -	Number One Canadian Infantry Battalion
#1 Can. F.D.S. -	Number One Canadian Field Dressing Station
#2 C.I.B. -	Number Two Canadian Infantry Battalion
#5 C.G.H. -	Number Five Canadian General Hospital
DUKW -	a type of amphibious water craft
#5 Fld. Amb. -	Number Five Field Ambulance
#9 Fld. Amb. -	Number Nine Field Ambulance
#2 F.S.U. -	Number Two Field Surgical Unit
O.R. -	Operating Room
P.O.W.s -	Prisoners of War
R.A.P. -	Regimental Aid Post
R.C.A.M.C. -	Royal Canadian Army Medical Corps
R.T.U. -	Regimental Treatment Unit
R.T.U. -	Return to Unit

ACKNOWLEDGMENTS

Thank you to Heather Campbell and Latitude46 for realizing the potential of this book.

I appreciate the financial assistance of the OAC's Literary Creation Projects (Works for Publication) – Northern Competition and the Accessibility Fund: Project Support. These grants gave me life-altering validation for my many years of work on this book.

An excerpt of this work as "Letters Home" appeared in *White Water Journal* 8. 2 (1998): 8-11.

Special thanks to my editors, Isabel Huggan and Emma Jay who worked patiently to guide me toward my vision for this manuscript.

Thank you to Amy Sheppard-Boal who was my Beta Reader.

Thank you to my workshop leaders over the years: Janis Rapoport, David Helwig (d.), Donna Sinclair, Leon Rooke, Bronwyn Wallace (d.), Bonnie Burnard (d.), Carol Shields (d.), Timothy Findley (d.), Richard Ford, and Marina Endicott, my FDU mentors: Walter Cummins, Rene Steinke, Renee Ashley, and David Grand and my late-in-life Nipissing University English professors: George Zytaruk (d.), Peter Clanfield, Gyllie Philipps, Laurie Kruk-McCulloch, and Denis Stokes. Thanks again for the pleasure I had in studying with you and for what I learned.

I am forever grateful for the continued friendship and support from Carole Malyon, Thea Caplan, and Barry Grills, fellow members of Leon Rooke's Kingston School for Writers' class, starting with that very hot summer so long ago.

Thanks to my Besta (Grandmother), Alma McConnell (d.) and

Aunt Lucille Berry (d.) for saving my father's letters, written home from WWII, which were guides for the letters I wrote to appear here.

Thanks to Maryellen Charrette for reading and transcribing the physician's hand in his letters.

My appreciation to Canada's National Archives for help with the WWII Italian Campaign's War Diaries, which record the R.C.A.M.C.'s journey from Sicily to the liberation of Holland.

Love and thanks to the WWW (Women Writers' Workshop) members: Jennifer Barbeau, Catherine Dean, and Laurie Kruk-McCulloch who met with me for 10 years before Covid19 hit.

Thanks to The Conspiracy of 3 Reading Series' originators Gil McElroy, Ian McCulloch (d.), Ken Stange (d.) and its members, in particular Tim & Karin Robertson, Bill Walton, John Novack, Gailand & Joyce McQueen, Sarah Winters, Tricia Mills, Sarah Carlin-Ball, John Jantunen, Tanja Rabe and Katerina Fretwell who have met for over thirty years, including virtually during Covid-19. My apologies to those I neglected to mention. You know who you are.

Thank you to Liz Lott, photographer, Sheena Wilton-Long, makeup artist, and Tony Cesarano, hairdresser, for their extraordinary work on my photograph.

Love and much thanks to my family: Frank, Nikoline, and Katie Calcaterra and Martin Holmes, Maryann McConnell, James McConnell, Sandra Martin, and Grandma Jean McConnell (d.), Rena Absher and Robert Calcaterra who never doubted, throughout twenty-five years of work, that this book would be published.